# DR. MADDEN'S MARRIAGE SOLUTION

ALISON ROBERTS

Recycling programs for this product may not exist in your area.

ISBN-13: 978-1-335-99367-0

Dr. Madden's Marriage Solution



This is a work of fiction. Names, characters, places and incidents are either the product of the author's imagination or are used fictitiously. Any resemblance to actual persons, living or dead, businesses, companies, events or locales is entirely coincidental.

For questions and comments about the quality of this book, please contact us at CustomerService@Harlequin.com.

Harlequin Enterprises ULC
22 Adelaide St. West, 41st Floor
Toronto, Ontario M5H 4E3, Canada
www.Harlequin.com

HarperCollins Publishers
Macken House, 39/40 Mayor Street Upper,
Dublin 1, D01 C9W8, Ireland
www.HarperCollins.com

**Printed in U.S.A.**

1 2 3 4 5 6 7 8 9 10 HDC 28 27 26 25

**Aratika Air Rescue**

*Hearts in critical condition!*

Buckle up and take flight with the team of dedicated medics at the Aratika Air Rescue base. Daring rescues and heart-stopping emergencies are just another day at the office for this crew. They'll risk it all to save their patients.

Yet, behind the flashing lights and roaring helicopter blades lies an undeniable truth. There's one thing these courageous doctors and paramedics *won't* risk: their hearts! But just when they think they've conquered every danger, love sends them into a tailspin they never saw coming...

Don't miss...

Nate & Alice's story
*Dr. Madden's Marriage Solution*

Available now!

And look out for...

Jules & Louis's story
and
Joel & Leah's story

Both coming soon!

Dear Reader,

I lived in New Zealand's capital, Wellington, for a few years. It was a long time ago, but the memories live on because it's a city that doesn't do things by half.

It's the gateway to the North Island and the link to the South, and it's famous for its weather. It can be so windy that passengers will clap when a pilot gets a plane safely onto the runway. The central city is surrounded by steep hills and even the views can be really spectacular with a drowned, volcanic crater forming its sparkling harbor.

It was the perfect setting for my Aratika Rescue Base that I dreamed up a few years ago, so I could throw my characters into all sorts of drama, both professional and personal.

I'm really happy to be revisiting both Aratika and Wellington, and here's the first of a new series—Nate and Alice's story. I really hope you enjoy it.

Happy reading!

With love

*Alison* xxx

**Alison Roberts** has been lucky enough to live in the South of France for several years recently but is now back in her home country of New Zealand. She is also lucky enough to write for the Harlequin Medical Romance line. A primary school teacher in a former life, she later became a qualified paramedic. She loves to travel and dance, drink champagne, and spend time with her daughter and her friends. Alison Roberts is the author of over one hundred books!

**Books by Alison Roberts**

**Harlequin Medical Romance**

***A Tale of Two Midwives***

*Falling for Her Forbidden Flatmate*
*Miracle Twins to Heal Them*

***Coastside ER***

*A Family Made in the ER*
*Single Dad for the Daredevil Doctor*

***Daredevil Doctors***

*Forbidden Nights with the Paramedic*
*Rebel Doctor's Baby Surprise*

***Royal York Hospital***

*Single Dad's Christmas Wish*

*City Vet, Country Temptation*
*Paramedic's Reunion in Paradise*
*Midwife's Three-Date Rule*
*Their Fake Date Rescue*

Visit the Author Profile page at Harlequin.com for more titles.

# CHAPTER ONE

'FOR GOD'S SAKE, ALICE... What's *taking* so long?'

Flight paramedic Alice Barlow's gaze swerved from the central clip on the strap that had been holding a defibrillator safely in place on its shelf during their flight to meet the incredulous stare of her crew partner.

She'd been out of her harness to grab the vital piece of equipment within a heartbeat of the helicopter skids making contact with the grass of this small town's football field. She didn't need to be glared at by a HEMS doctor, who was also the senior medic on this crew, to be reminded of how urgent this response was.

A baby who had stopped breathing for long enough to turn blue? Who had started breathing again when his panicked mother grabbed him from the floor, only to cough so hard he'd made himself sick? The ambulance dispatch technician had been able to hear the sound of the baby's severe respiratory distress on the phone call. This was quite possibly a life-or-death call-out. It was also the worst time a clip could have malfunctioned and be refusing to release.

'It's jammed,' Alice said tersely.

Nate's arm shot past her. He squeezed the sides of the clip and tugged but it still wasn't budging. With a muttered but audible curse, he dropped the arm loop of the kit he was holding and used both his hands to give the plastic clip enough of a wrench to snap whatever part of the mechanism had jammed. Alice reached for the handle of the vital piece of equipment but Nate was faster.

'I've got it. You take the kit.' He shoved the pack towards her with his foot as he used his free hand to reach for an oxygen cylinder.

Their crewman was sliding the side door open. This was a hot landing, where their pilot, Andy, would keep the helicopter idling, ready for a rapid departure. Those minutes saved could be what made the difference in getting a fragile patient to definitive critical care.

Alice was looking at Nate's back as she kept her head down and moved swiftly to get past the danger zone of moving rotors. A glance over her shoulder earned a 'thumbs up' from Andy, the pilot, who'd been watching to make sure he knew exactly where she was and that she was safe. Now she could increase her speed to catch up with Nate, who hadn't even glanced over his shoulder to see where she was.

What was up with him today?

It felt like more than the stress of a kind of call-out that would put any medic on edge. Nate had been noticeably distant ever since he'd arrived for his shift at the Aratika Rescue Base. Grim, even. And, okay, everyone had been cutting him some slack recently because they knew he'd had some personal issues going on but this was on a whole new level.

Alice hadn't seen even a hint of a smile today and now he was snapping at her for something that wasn't her fault? This wasn't like the Nathaniel Madden she had been working with for a long time now. Something was up but now wasn't the time to think about it, let alone try and discover what was going on, so she pushed her concern very firmly out of her head.

A woman with grey hair was waving frantically at them and pointing to a car parked behind her with all its doors wide open. As they got closer, Alice could see a woman sitting on the back seat, a baby clutched in her arms. She was rocking the bundle and she was sobbing.

Alice could feel her heart dropping like a stone.

Were they too late?

'Oh…thank goodness you're here.' The older woman looked close to tears herself.

'What's happening?' Nate asked. 'Has baby stopped breathing again?'

'No...but we keep expecting him to. I'm his grandma.' The woman pressed a hand to her mouth, catching Alice's gaze as Nate stepped past her and crouched in front of the sobbing mother.

'I'm Alice,' she said.

It wasn't like Nate not to introduce himself, either, with his ability to connect and form instant bonds with anybody on scene, from the patient and their family to any local medics or emergency service personnel. Onlookers, even, that he might want to get rid of.

'And that's Nate,' she added, to cover the omission. 'One of our HEMS doctors.' She tried to convey reassurance without saying out loud that this baby was lucky because Nate had to be the best emergency specialist she had ever worked with in her many years as a paramedic.

Another step took her close enough to see past Nate's broad back. He was doing an initial assessment, talking calmly at the same time.

'This is baby Max, yes? And you're his mum, Louise, is that right?'

'Yes...' The woman started lifting her baby, desperate to give him to someone who could help.

'You keep holding Max for a minute,' Nate told her. 'It will help to keep him warm and he's less likely to get distressed, which will make it easier for me to see what's going on and get some baseline recordings. As soon as we know he's stable enough, we'll get him to hospital.'

'And I'll be able to go with him?'

'We'll talk about that soon. We need to focus on Max for the moment.'

He glanced sideways at Alice, who was right beside him now. She had put down the large red bag with all its internal and external pockets. She was already opening the zip on the airway pocket because she could hear this baby gasping for air at a rate that was well over the upper limit of normal and, even without a stethoscope, it was easy to hear the crackles and wheeze of obstructed airways. He was going to need oxygen. Medication. Possibly intubation if he became too tired or his level of consciousness was dropping.

And, if that was the case, with a critically ill baby on a ventilator, his mother was unlikely to be allowed to travel with them in the helicopter. As hard as it was, they would need the space and focus to do their job. A terrified mother distracting them was a complication it was best to avoid.

'Let's get some oxygen on with nasal prongs,' Nate said. He lifted his stethoscope from where it was hanging around his neck and fitted the earpieces. 'We need an oxygen saturation level, too, please.'

Alice fitted the soft plastic nozzles into the baby's nostrils, using a piece of tape to secure the tubing. The baby looked as if he wanted to cry but the effort was just too much. His skin was very pale but there were mottled red patches on his cheeks.

'So Max has been sick for a couple of days?' Nate tilted his head as he pulled the earpieces of his stethoscope clear.

'Yes…' Louise was still sniffing but she'd stopped crying. She looked almost as pale as her baby. 'There's been a nasty bug going around school and Max's big sister is sick at the moment.'

Alice turned the oxygen cylinder on. She also took a paediatric bag mask out of the kit so she could be ready if Max deteriorated any further and needed help with his breathing. Babies were scary to treat because they could compensate well for a time to cope with challenges like a lack of oxygen or poor circulation but then they could crash with an alarming speed and depth.

'Has he been feeding normally?'

'No… He's been coughing too much today to even suck properly.'

Alice caught the flick of Nate's glance as she wrapped the Velcro strap of a pulse oximeter around Max's tiny foot and she caught the silent communication instantly.

*'Don't refasten the leg domes on that onesie.'*

*'You want access for an intra-osseous line for IV?'*

*'He's dehydrated. Might be the quickest route.'*

The ease with which they could understand each other and work together had been there right from their first mission together. Nate only did one or two twelve-hour shifts per week—the rest of his working time was spent in the emergency department of Wellington's largest hospital as a consultant emergency medicine specialist. Alice had never asked, but had often wondered, if Nate had gone to the manager of the Aratika Rescue Base and put in a request to work with her on his shifts whenever possible after that first time, because it was very rare for her not to be his crew partner.

If he *had* made the request, it wouldn't have bothered Alice in the slightest because she knew it would have been purely for professional reasons. Nate was married. Alice was very happily single. Along with the way they could work together, perhaps that was the foundation for the firm friendship that had grown slowly over the last year. They were both completely safe from the kind of complications that working closely together in an often-fraught environment could so easily generate.

That silent exchange had done more than provide Alice with a flash of the strong bond she had with this colleague. She'd also been reminded of the reason why Nate might seem out of sorts today. He had separated from his wife weeks ago now. The reality of a shattered relationship would be sinking in and Alice knew, only too well, how hard that could be.

But that wasn't a thought that could be allowed to even form properly, like feeling hurt that he'd snapped at her earlier. What it did do was let Alice make allowances for any mood swing Nate might be experiencing and to let go of any concern that might disrupt her focus.

'Oxygen saturation 95 percent,' she relayed. 'No…make that 94.'

Far too low. And it was dropping, despite the level of supplemental oxygen the baby was now receiving. The effort of trying to breathe fast enough to increase blood levels of the vital gas had to be exhausting this tiny person.

She could feel the vibration of the helicopter in the ground beneath her feet. The sooner they could get airborne the better because they could deliver Max into the expert hands of paediatric specialists within half an hour but they couldn't leave until they had a stable airway. It would only take a small shift for this baby to lose the ability to pull in enough oxygen to stay alive, and the familiar prickle on the back of her neck was a warning that it might well turn out to be a difficult task to stabilise and then transfer this patient.

And her intuition proved correct. That shift

occurred only minutes later, as Nate was taping a protective shield over the intra-osseous line he had placed.

Max stopped breathing again.

'Okay, Louise,' Nate said calmly. 'I need to take Max now.'

He was slipping his hands under the baby, as he spoke, to take him from his mother's arms and put him down on the clean towel Alice had spread to lay out items they might need. By the time Nate laid the limp form of the baby on the ground and positioned him to make sure his airway was open, she had the small bag mask in her hands. She connected it to the oxygen supply, covered the mouth and nose with a tight seal, and puffed oxygen in gently, watching the chest rise and fall.

For Louise, who was now standing with her mother's arms around her, watching the resuscitation in horror, it must have looked like things were moving too fast to process. Nate's hands were flashing from one checklist point to another, pulling clear plastic kits from where they were fastened inside the pack and ripping open zips. He had the contents of the airway cube set out and was drawing up the drugs to induce sedation and then paralyse the baby so that they could take over his airway and breathing.

Andy was still inside the idling helicopter but

the crewman, Nick, who was trained to be able to assist in situations like this, had joined them and knelt beside Alice to take over responsibility for using the bag mask.

Alice stuck the adhesive patches onto the front and back of Max's chest. With their inbuilt electrodes and wires, they could be used for both monitoring heart rate and rhythm and to deliver a shock for defibrillation if necessary. She double-checked the drugs that Nate was drawing up and made sure that all the gear they might need was readily available, like suction and alternative airways and even a surgical pack for the worst-case scenario of *can't intubate, can't oxygenate*.

Seconds later, Nate had a video laryngoscope in his hands and Alice was ready to provide an extra set of hands to position and steady the baby's head, remove the guidewire and help secure the breathing tube when Nate had confirmed its correct placement.

Now they needed to get the baby on board the helicopter. Nate was making sure lines and wires were secure and not tangled, getting ready to pick Max up and carry him while Alice and Nick were stuffing the rest of their gear back into the kit. He was also telling Louise and her mother what was about to happen.

'We'll take Max straight to the paediatric department in Wellington General,' he told them.

'We'll be in contact with the specialists as we're flying so they'll be ready and waiting for us.'

'But…' Louise let go of her mum's hand to touch her baby's head. 'But I can come with him, can't I?'

Alice stuck the clear-sided pack with IV supplies back into the kit by attaching the Velcro patches to each other. Her heart was sinking because she knew that Nate had no choice in what he was about to say.

'I'm very sorry. We're going to have him on a ventilator for his breathing and there will be too much going on for extra passengers to be able to be onboard.'

There was all the warmth and sympathy in Nate's tone that Alice had come to expect, so why did she have the impression that he was still keeping his distance?

That something else was on his mind, at a time when it really, really shouldn't be?

'I'll drive you,' Louise's mother said firmly. 'Come on… We need to let the doctors do what they need to do. We'll get going right now and we won't be that far behind. John can bring everything we need later.' She put her arm around the distraught young mother as she turned her back towards their car.

Nate might be unusually distant, Alice decided, as they got back on board, but it wasn't putting their patient at any risk. They worked fast, hooking Max up to the portable ventilator, making sure all the monitoring equipment was functioning and stowing other gear so they could take off safely.

'Oxygen saturation's 99 percent,' Alice noted aloud, happy with such a big improvement in a vital sign. They had done their job, securing an airway and taking over the work of breathing from an exhausted infant. They were in the air again and on their way to where little Max needed to be. She expected at least a nod of satisfaction from Nate, if not a smile and a look that acknowledged her part in the management of this emergency.

But there was no response from Nate. He was in the seat closest to the stretcher that had the paediatric bassinet attached to it. Baby Max was strapped inside the bassinet, with the tubes and wires of his monitoring equipment carefully secured around him. The ventilator and defibrillator had flashing lights, measurements that were automatically updating and a cardiac graph running constantly across the screen, the spikes close together due to the infant's rapid heart rate.

Nate's gaze was fixed to the screen, as if he was expecting an alarm to start sounding at any moment and indicate a new crisis. It was as if he hadn't even heard Alice, which was impossible because the microphones and headphones built into their helmets made communication crystal-clear. Intimate almost, when you could feel the vibration of someone's voice on the delicate skin of your ear.

And that made his nonresponse to Alice feel like a deliberate snub.

Was she missing something, here? Had she done something to upset Nate?

She tried to retrace the timeline of their day so far. It had been a relatively quiet shift before this with only one call-out, to a medical practice in a small coastal town too far away from a hospital to make road transport acceptable for a man with chest pain and clear signs of an evolving heart attack visible on the ECG. The middle-aged man had needed pain relief and oxygen but it had been a completely straightforward mission with no complications, and their patient had been relaxed enough to have a conversation with Nate about his passion for fishing.

With the information being transmitted directly to the cardiology team at the receiving hospital, they were waiting on the rooftop helipad to whisk the man straight to the catheter laboratory where his blocked arteries could be treated. They were back on base by lunchtime to find that their devoted, volunteer housekeeper, Shirley, had made a stack of cheese and onion toasted sandwiches and everybody had been delighted.

*You're a star, Shirley*, Andy had said. *Nobody makes a toastie as good as you do.*

Shirley had flapped her hand at him. *Flattery will get you everywhere, young man.*

Alice could remember the laughter around the table. But she also realised she hadn't seen Nate eating one of those delicious sandwiches. He'd excused himself when his phone rang and went to take the call in private. Had Nate noticed the meaningful glances that had been exchanged between his colleagues as he walked away, perhaps? The ones that were conveying hope that this might be the start of sorting out whatever had gone so wrong in his marriage?

But Juliette—one of the base's motorbike paramedics—had shaken her head slowly, when someone observed that he'd been gone a long time and maybe that was a positive sign.

*I wouldn't hold your breath*, she'd said quietly. *If it is a call from Donna, I don't think it'll be good news. I heard this morning that she's heading for Europe. And that she's not travelling alone*.

Alice had found herself avoiding eye contact with Nate when he came back. It wasn't that they'd been gossiping, exactly. No one had asked any questions about who Donna's travelling companion might be but the inference that she was leaving with another man had been inescapable, and Alice had been embarrassed that she now knew more than she wanted to know about his marriage.

It seemed easier to join dots now. What if Nate was aware that the fact his wife had left him for someone else could have become common knowledge? What if he'd only just become aware of it himself? That could have been what had tipped the balance prior to his shift today, couldn't it? He'd been subdued for weeks now but there was an uncharacteristic edge of something like anger in his demeanour today.

And Alice, as his crew partner, was on the front line for feeling the brunt of it, and hanging around on base without the distraction of any call-outs this afternoon could well have exacerbated an emotional reaction to something that was happening away from a professional arena.

That didn't make any of it okay, though. There was an unspoken rule that personal issues had to be left at the hangar door on this base. Letting them interfere with team dynamics, or worse, patient care was completely unacceptable and Alice found that her eyes were narrowing as she watched Nate watching the monitors. Maybe she needed to have a word with Nate to let him know that she'd been affected today. That, if he couldn't be sure it wasn't going to happen again, he might need to take some time away from work.

The sudden beeping of an alarm was magnified by coming through the microphone on Nate's helmet.

'Crew harness off.' Nate's voice was as crisp as the click of releasing the clip on his harness. He braced himself against the stretcher and had his stethoscope in his ears as he leaned over the bassinette.

The alarm was still sounding. The oxygen saturation had dropped below the set parameters. It was still dropping as Alice unclipped her own harness.

'Crew harness off,' she said, to alert Andy that she was about to move.

'Roger that.' He knew they wouldn't be taking the risk of being unsecured in any unexpected turbulence unless it was unavoidable. He would be able to hear the alarm going off as clearly as she could.

Max looked as white as the rolled-up towels that cushioned the sides of the bassinette. Nate had the disk of his stethoscope on the tiny chest, intently focussed on what he was hearing,

'Heart rate's dropping,' Alice warned. 'Under a hundred.'

The oxygen saturation was still dropping. Alice's mouth went dry. 'O2 sats under ninety.'

Nate's gaze flicked up to the screen. 'Andy? What's our ETA?'

'Seven minutes.'

Alice looked at Max. His fingertips were dark and his lips, around the device holding the breathing tube in place, were visible enough to see that they were blue.

'Right-sided breath sounds absent,' Nate said, his voice grim. 'He's bradycardic and blood pressure's falling.'

Alice knew what was happening. Possibly due to the underlying respiratory illness and severe coughing or the pressures of the ventilator, damage had occurred to a tiny lung and air was filling the chest cavity to create a situation that would stop both the lungs and heart functioning. They couldn't wait for the seven minutes to get to their destination. They only had a matter of seconds to deal with this crisis before it turned into a full-blown resuscitation for a cardiac arrest.

'I'm going to do a needle decompression.'

Nate's calm statement was for Andy's benefit. As a medivac pilot, he knew how important it would be to keep the aircraft as stable as possible when an invasive procedure was happening. He would be lowering their speed, avoiding any turns or pitch changes and watching out for turbulence that could be avoided.

Alice hadn't missed Nate's choice of words,

however. Did he really think he was about to do this entirely by himself?

She braced herself with one hand as she grabbed an IV kit, ripping open the zip.

Nate was pulling on a pair of gloves. 'Find me a twenty-two-gauge cannula, thanks, Alice.'

She put an alcohol wipe down beside his hand. He turned his head.

'Cannula.' It was a clearly enunciated command, not a request. It felt like a reprimand that she hadn't provided what he'd asked for fast enough. She peeled back the top of the sealed package containing the cannula so he could take it out by its base.

Alice watched as Nate gently touched the notch of the baby's neck, went straight down and then sideways to find the exact spot between those miniature ribs to insert the needle and reach the air pocket. She held her breath, sending out a silent plea to the universe not to send a bump of turbulence in their direction for the next few seconds but by the time she'd formed the thought, Nate's hand was out, wanting the syringe she was holding so that he could attach it to the end of the cannula. Nate pulled back the plunger, emptied the syringe and repeated the action.

'Sat's coming up.' It felt like the first breath Alice had taken in some time but she let it out again almost immediately in a sigh of relief.

'Ninety-one…ninety-two…' The heart rate was also increasing. She waited for Nate to catch her gaze. Like he always did in that moment when they knew they'd won.

But he had his stethoscope in place again and the only person he was looking at was baby Max.

'Strap back in.' Andy's voice came through their headphones, moments later. 'We're about to land.'

They were late back to base after delivering their patient to the paediatric intensive care unit before making the changeover from their portable equipment, partly because they waited until a chest drain was inserted to ensure that another pneumothorax couldn't accumulate.

Both Alice and Nate were drained enough, after such a challenging retrieval, for it to excuse the communication that was confined to totally practical requests or instructions.

*'Find a three-millimetre ETT tube while you're there, will you?'*

*'The lifepack needs new patches.'*

*'And fresh batteries.'*

*'Swap out that oxygen tank for a new one.'*

*'Sign off these RSI drugs with me, will you?'*

They tidied up, cleaned gear and restocked everything they'd used.

It was well past time they both went home and

Alice was about to open the side door in the hangar that led to the car park but she could hear the sound of Nate's boots on the concrete right behind her and, at the last moment, she dropped her hand and turned around to face him.

She couldn't leave things like this. She wouldn't be seeing Nate for another week and she didn't want to be overthinking what had gone down today.

She was blocking Nate's exit. He raised his eyebrows, clearly expecting her to step aside. Instead, she folded her arms.

'What was that all about today, Nate? What is it I'm supposed to have done?'

'What on earth are you talking about?'

'Don't pretend you don't know.' Alice glared at him. 'You snapped at me as if I was hell-bent on making it as difficult as possible for you to do your job. It wasn't *my* fault that the clip broke. You didn't even hear me passing on information, or if you did, you just ignored me which is downright *rude*.' To her horror, Alice could feel the prickle of tears behind her eyes. It had been hurtful but, if he couldn't see that, she wasn't about to tell him. 'And, you know what?' she fired as a parting shot. 'You needed to use an alcohol wipe for skin prep, so it wasn't actually stupid to hand that to you before a cannula.'

Nate was staring back at her. He took a quick

glance over his shoulder as if he was checking that nobody was overhearing this rant.

'Are you suggesting I put someone at risk?'

'*No…*' Alice shook her head. 'I would have said something a lot sooner than this if I had. Clinically, you did your job as well as you always do. It was the way you took your bad mood out on me that…that…' she let her breath out in a sigh, the wind leaving her sails completely as she saw the way Nate put his hand to his forehead, rubbing at the lines that had deepened as he scrunched up his face '…wasn't nice,' she finished with a shrug. 'That's all.'

She was turning to the door again.

Letting it go.

But the sincerity in Nate's voice made her pause.

'I'm sorry, Alice.'

'Okay…' She was quite prepared to accept an apology. She didn't want this to be hanging in the air the next time they worked together. She glanced up at him. 'I know you've got stuff going on.'

Nate's eyes were so dark they almost looked as brown as hers even though she knew perfectly well that they were blue.

'You don't know the half of it,' he muttered.

*Oh*…the note in Nate's voice now sounded like very real pain. Maybe they'd only ever been colleagues but there was a solid friendship there as well. They trusted each other implicitly when it came to anything professional. Suddenly, it felt like a barrier needed to be broken. That Nate needed someone in a very personal corner of his life.

The urge to put her arms around him and offer comfort came from nowhere and it was strong enough to be disturbing, so Alice stayed very still.

'What's really going on, Nate?' she asked quietly. 'Is this because Donna's leaving?'

Nate was silent for a heartbeat. And then another. He was still holding her gaze and, when he broke the silence, his voice was raw.

'It's bigger than that,' he said. 'A lot bigger.'

Alice waited. She was here. If he wanted to tell her, he would.

He did.

'I'm going to be a father,' he said. 'And I don't have the faintest idea how I'm going to cope…'

# CHAPTER TWO

THE SHOCK OF Nate's words was stunning.

Alice couldn't quite get her head around them.

'Donna's *pregnant*?'

'No.'

'You mean…someone *else* is pregnant?' Alice lowered her voice even though they were still alone in the hangar. 'With *your* baby?'

Stupid question. Of course that was what he meant but this was even more shocking than knowing his wife was leaving him and taking his unborn baby with her. This meant that Nate must have cheated on Donna and maybe given her just cause to walk out on him? Had everyone on-base been offering sympathy and cutting him some slack if he wasn't as nice to be around as usual when he had, in fact, brought this all on himself? The thought came and went in the space of a single heartbeat, followed by another flash that was just as fleeting.

No… Despite the fact that she had been blind-sided by her last boyfriend doing exactly that to *her*—it simply didn't fit the man who Alice thought she knew. A loyal, honourable, passionate man who was, outwardly at least, devoted to his work and his family, presumably including the future children that she knew he looked forward to welcoming. For heaven's sake, hadn't she seen Nate poring over a real estate magazine just a couple of months ago, saying that he and Donna were looking to change their apartment lifestyle for a more family-friendly property?

Nate must have seen the shock in her eyes, possibly being washed away by the disbelief. Had that morphed into disappointment, perhaps? Was it actually possible he was just another man who could charm women into trusting them enough to be planning their future around them and then leave them picking up the pieces when they'd realised what a terrible mistake it had been? Like the bad choices Alice had made more than once?

Oddly, a reflection of her own shock was written all over Nate's face.

'It's *not* what you're thinking.' His tone was urgent.

Alice added confusion into how she was feeling. 'What is it, then?'

'It's...' Nate blew out a breath '...complicated.'

Alice's breath came out in a huff that bordered on laughter. 'I'll bet it is.' She wanted to shake her head and say something that might come across as less than sympathetic but then she saw the look in Nate's eyes.

A look that was dark enough to be desperation?

This man was her colleague. Her friend. And he was in trouble.

'Do you want to talk about it?' Her words were tentative but she was holding his gaze, hoping he could see that she was prepared to shelve any judgement. That she had the time to listen and maybe offer at least some kind of support.

Nate looked over his shoulder again. 'Not here.'

Alice looked at her watch. 'It's way past dinner time,' she said. 'Why don't we meet at that pub we always go to for work-related celebrations? You came to the drinks after work for Andy's birthday last month, remember?'

'The Irish pub? In Petone?'

'That's the one. The Emerald Harp. Traffic won't be a problem at this time of night, the food's good and we're almost regulars.'

No eyebrows would be raised that crew members from the base might be grabbing a bite to eat together, as a form of debriefing after a long day or a big job.

Nate looked like he was going to back off fast. Alice fully expected him to thank her but say something like it was no big deal and she probably had much better things to be doing with her time away from work.

'You never know,' she added. 'I might be able to help.' She could feel her lips curve into what was undoubtedly a cheeky smile. 'You know how bossy I can be. Giving people ideas about how they can solve problems is possibly one of my best splinter skills.'

It was nearly fifteen minutes later when Nate followed Alice's vehicle into the entrance of The Emerald Harp's car park.

He cut his engine but didn't open his door immediately because he needed to close his eyes for a moment and pull in a deep breath. He'd been arguing with himself for the whole drive from the base. Did he really want to talk about this? To share details of his private life with someone who was not really anything more than a colleague?

Okay, shoving Alice into a purely professional category wasn't entirely fair. He genuinely enjoyed both working with her and hanging out with her on the base when they weren't working. It wasn't as if they chose to spend time together away from the work they shared, aside from work-related gatherings, of course, like Andy's birthday drinks but that was just the way things were. Donna had left her job as a nurse years ago. The last thing she wanted to do when they had time off together was to hang around with medics who, invariably, started talking shop.

But did that mean that he and Alice weren't really friends?

It was as close to a friendship as any that Nate currently had in his life. He had his work at the hospital, his work at the rescue base and…his marriage. That was his life. Or it had been until a few short weeks ago.

Right now he felt cast adrift, utterly lost, and he knew that the worst was still to come. He also knew that personal information anyone would prefer to keep private was already circulating like wildfire on the kind of grapevine that work establishments like hospitals were notorious for. It was more than likely that Alice had already heard rumours. Maybe the only real control he had over what was turning his life inside out was to make sure at least one person other than himself knew the truth.

And why not Alice Barlow?

He could see her getting out of her car and walking towards him now and she looked like she always did. Dark, wavy hair pulled back into a ponytail, average height, her curvy figure more obvious in civvies than the base uniform. A confident, intelligent, sometimes opinionated and often funny woman who was passionate about her career. She was also a very kind person. Nate had seen evidence of that time and again and it went a long way to explain why she was such a popular member of the Aratika staff.

Perhaps a bit of kindness was exactly what he needed right now. Or company? It had been a bit of a wake-up call to find that this unfamiliar territory he was trying to navigate was a rather overwhelmingly lonely space.

Nate got out of his car to find himself staring at the bright green harp on the pub's signage with a tagline below that he hadn't noticed on his first visit.

*Every song tells its own story.*

One side of his mouth tilted in a wry smile. Yeah… He had his own story and if he couldn't tell it to someone as trustworthy as Alice it might stay untold forever. Simmering beneath the surface and becoming a toxic brew that could turn him into a person nobody would want to talk to.

He might end up being locked into this lonely space totally alone.

And who would want that?

It was all dark, polished wood and pools of lamplight that made glass sparkle behind the bar. Irish music played in the background but it was midweek and missing the crowds and noise level of the nights they had a live band in the house, like the last time they'd been here.

'Can I get you something to drink?'

They were in a puddle of light and Alice could see that Nate's face had lightened a little since that intense moment in the hangar before she'd asked if he wanted to talk about whatever was going on. His eyes looked blue again. A very dark blue that made him look as if he could be of Irish descent himself with how dark his hair was. Hair that was ruffled enough now to remind her that running his fingers through it was a sure sign that he was stressed.

'Yes, please,' Alice said.

'What would you like?'

'What are you going to have?'

'Has to be Guinness, given where we are. I go for quality over quantity, so I'm thinking Foreign Extra Stout.'

Alice threw a smile at the bartender waiting to take their order. She'd just thought of the perfect way to let Nate know that she was here for him. Ready to listen. And help, if she could.

'I'll have what he's having,' she told the bartender.

She turned back in time to catch Nate's eyebrows lifting.

'What…do you have a problem with women drinking Guinness?'

'Not at all. Are you aware that the Foreign Extra is known as the blackest, boldest Guinness there is?'

Oops. Alice didn't normally drink any beer other than a pale lager on a hot summer's day but she couldn't back out now. She tried a casual shrug.

'You mean you've been working with me all this time and you didn't know that Bold was my middle name?'

Nate gave his head a small shake but he was smiling for the first time today and that made Alice relax a little. She had to admit that being here in Nate's company was feeling more awkward than she'd expected. Maybe it was because they were alone together in a social situation? It was quite possible there were people here that might recognise them. Nate might be separated from his wife but he was still a married man and sometimes people couldn't help jumping to conclusions that might be totally wrong but still had the power to do some damage.

She picked up one of the laminated menus on the bar and scanned it as the inky liquid was being poured from bottles to fill their glasses beneath a layer of brownish foam.

'I'm *so* hungry,' she said aloud.

'Me, too,' Nate said. 'What looks good?'

'Well, I don't know about you, but I can't go past a good slow-cooked beef hotpot.'

'Perfect match for your drinks.' The bartender

nodded approvingly. 'That hotpot's got Guinness in it, too.'

It was Nate's turn to smile as he reached to pick up the tulip-shaped glasses. 'I'll have what she's having,' he said.

He led the way to a table in a corner booth and they sat facing each other. They both picked up their glasses. Alice took a cautious sip. Her head jerked up to find that Nate had yet to taste his drink. He was watching her over the rim of his glass.

'Oh…' Alice put her glass down and eyed it with respect.

'You don't like it?'

'I'm not sure,' Alice confessed.

'First time?' Nate's lips twitched. 'I did wonder.'

'I'm being bold,' Alice said. She picked up her glass again and took another, very small sip. 'How do they do it?' she asked. 'Do they go and find random barbecues and scrape all that burnt, black stuff off the bottom of the tray and throw it in with the normal brew?'

Nate actually laughed aloud. The sound went past Alice's ears to flow right through her body and it was impossible not to smile back at him. This felt like a win. The amusement had made his eyes crinkle and his face relax and she could almost forget how desperate he'd looked back in the hangar, but the silence that fell after the laughter faded was full of so many questions it felt almost solid.

Alice didn't need to ask any of them yet, however. Catching her bottom lip between her teeth as she met Nate's gaze was enough of a prompt.

'It's a long story,' he said. 'Are you sure you want to hear it?'

'That's why I'm here,' she responded. She tilted her head towards her glass. 'And I reckon that drink's going to last me for hours given that half a mil at a time is more than enough.'

'No one's waiting for you to get home?'

'No.' Alice didn't offer any more information. This wasn't supposed to be about her.

Maybe Nate hadn't got the memo.

'How old are you, Alice?'

'Thirty-six.'

'Have you ever been married?'

'No.' Alice made a face. 'Don't intend to, either. In fact, I think I'm over men. Been there, done that. Not going to keep the T-shirt.'

Nate opened his mouth as if he was about to ask another question but then closed it with a firmness that suggested he'd thought better of it. Because he knew he could be stepping, uninvited, onto sensitive ground?

'I got married before I even hit the big three-oh,' he told her. 'That's more than ten years ago.

My friends were settling down—some of them had started having kids and I'd always seen that as part of my own future.' He was watching a waitress coming towards their table from the kitchens, carrying a tray. 'I was an only child,' he added. 'I'd always thought the one thing that would make life perfect was to have a big family.'

Alice grimaced. 'I was an only child, too,' she told him, 'but I thought the one thing that would make life perfect was not to have a family at all.'

She got a distinctly curious glance this time but they both leaned back as rustic, ceramic ramekins were placed on the table. The thin, overlapping slices of potato on the top were crisp and brown and the escaping steam smelled rich and delicious. The cutlery was wrapped in serviettes and there was a small basket of bread rolls.

'Be careful,' the waitress warned. 'That hotpot's like lava at the moment.'

Alice's stomach rumbled but having broken the potato layer with her fork, she knew it would be unwise to taste it yet. Nate hadn't even unwrapped his cutlery and the look he was giving Alice now was almost a frown, as if he was worried about something. What was it she'd said? Oh, yeah. That she was over men and didn't want a family.

'Don't get me wrong,' she said. 'I don't hate men. I'd even be up for finding a life partner—

I just don't want kids. I've found guys who *say* they don't want kids but then it turns out that they're just filling in time until they can find someone who wants to have their babies. Or that's how it feels. I've given up looking.'

'At least you're upfront about not wanting them,' Nate said. 'It's something that everyone should at least talk about before making any kind of commitment.'

'Did you?'

Nate nodded. 'It was something we both wanted, right from the start. We were young. We were both going to work hard for a few years and save a deposit for a big, family house and then start having those babies. At least three. Maybe five.'

Nate paused to take a first, tentative bite of his still steaming dinner. Alice followed his example and found beef that had been cooked long enough to melt in her mouth. She ripped a chunk off a bread roll to dip in the thick gravy.

'This is *so* good… Wish I could cook like this.'

For a while, they both ate in a companionable silence but Nate slowed down and was simply playing with his fork before he'd finished his meal, as if his appetite had suddenly disappeared.

Finally he put his fork down and leaned back in his chair. 'I guess the real start of my story was a couple of years later. Donna's mother rang to tell her that one of her cousin's kids had just been diagnosed with a syndrome. Have you heard of fragile X syndrome?'

Alice shook her head, not trying to pretend that she'd heard of it but forgotten the details. Nate had never judged Alice on any gaps in her medical knowledge. He seemed to enjoy teaching her something new and she always enjoyed listening.

'It's the most common cause of inherited intellectual disability. It affects boys more than girls, can range from mild to severe and there's no cure. An affected child might need lifelong therapy and support services.'

There was almost a roughness to Nate's voice that made this feel very different to any of those bite-sized tutorials related to a profession they were both passionate about. This information was significant.

'Nobody had even known it was in the family,' Nate continued. 'The doctor involved advised that any close relatives who were planning to have children should be tested—just in case.' He paused to take in a slow breath. 'Turned out Donna is a carrier.'

'Oh, *no…*' Alice felt guilty for entertaining the thought that Nate might have cheated on his wife. Of course there had to have been more to this story. 'That must have been such a shock.'

'The genetic counsellors were great. There

were ways around it. It's possible to test prenatally from about ten weeks' gestation but…' Nate pulled in a breath. 'It's a 50 percent chance of it being bad news and neither of us were happy with the idea of having to make a decision about whether to terminate a pregnancy on the grounds of having a potentially severely disabled child.'

Alice nodded. That was understandable.

'There were other options. We could think about adoption. Or go the IVF route where the embryos were tested before implantation and only the unaffected ones used but that's quite a major medical journey and I couldn't blame Donna for needing time to get used to the idea. We got on with our lives in the meantime but…something had changed. The dream wasn't going to be easy any longer and it seemed to have a flow-on effect on the rest of our lives.' Nate shrugged. 'It didn't seem to matter what I said—Donna still felt like it was her fault. We stopped talking about it. We kind of drifted apart. I was focussed on my specialist training and getting a consultancy. Donna did some part-time modelling and then she gave up nursing when she started to get noticed. We were both busy and happy enough, I guess, and another year or two went by.'

They'd both pushed their ramekins aside by now. Their waitress came back to collect them.

'Can I get you guys anything else? Dessert? Coffee?'

'I'd like a coffee, please,' Alice said. 'A flat white would be great.'

'Me, too,' Nate echoed.

He sighed as they were left alone again. 'I knew time was running out with us both nearly in our forties,' he said. 'So I brought it up again about the time I started shifts at Aratika. She said she wasn't sure she wanted to get pregnant anytime soon because it would be too disruptive for her modelling career. She loved the work and she was making more money than I was by that stage.' He shrugged. 'That was when I suggested surrogacy. I was really honest about how much it meant to me to have a family and I think we both knew it was an issue that could break us.'

He looked up and Alice was startled to see something that looked like guilt in his eyes.

'In retrospect, I can see this was partly a Band-Aid baby to try and save our marriage but, at the time, it was definitely what we both wanted. We found an online community and got all the information we needed. We were both excited about it. We made the decision to use a donor egg and my sperm and it turned out to be remarkably easy to find someone who was prepared to help us achieve our dream of having a baby. A gestational surrogate, who has no biological relationship to the baby they're carrying.'

'That's a huge thing for someone to do for a stranger.'

'It is,' Nate agreed. 'And Simone is just the loveliest person. A real "earth-mother" type. She and her partner live on an off-the-grid lifestyle block near the sea right at the bottom of the South Island and she home-schools their five kids. Family is everything to them and she absolutely loves being pregnant but they don't want any more of their own. She wanted to help others discover the joy of becoming a family and she'd been looking for the right couple for quite a while. She said she'd know when she found them and it turned out to be me and Donna. Everything was perfect.' He paused and then let his breath out slowly. 'Until it wasn't.'

'I know almost nothing about the process of surrogacy in New Zealand,' she admitted. 'But I've heard some horror stories about things that have happened overseas.'

'It is complicated,' Nate said. 'It's legal, but only if it's altruistic and the surrogate isn't making money out of it. There are all sorts of hoops to jump through, like meeting ethics committee criteria and getting approval for adoption.' He shook his head. 'That was weird for me, the idea of having to apply for permission to adopt my own child. Our laws state that the woman who gives birth to the child is its legal mother, even if she has no biological relationship to it.'

Alice's jaw dropped. 'Wow…that's a minefield.'

The lines of tension were back in Nate's face. She could see the muscles in his throat moving, as if it was suddenly hard to swallow.

'That's exactly what it is.' He rubbed the back of his neck. 'And maybe Donna stood on the first mine but I'm the one who's about to detonate an even bigger one.'

The arrival of their coffees broke Nate's story long enough for Alice to get her head around the enormity of what Nate had been through to get this far. But the story was far from over. What had happened for things to have gone so wrong? And what was about to happen next that Nate was so worried about?

She didn't even pick up her coffee cup because the question on the tip of her tongue was all-consuming.

'What happened, Nate? When did it start going wrong?'

He pushed his coffee cup further away. 'Reality happened,' he said quietly. 'I don't think any of us expected the first implantation to be successful but there we were. This wasn't an imaginary baby any longer. We were on the countdown to becoming parents and it was bigger than either of us anticipated. I was thrilled. Donna was… shocked. She might have been happy with the idea of us having children but she'd put her hand up to be a mother to someone *else's* child and it was only after she knew it was really going to happen that she began to realise that perhaps it wasn't actually something she wanted to do.' He cleared his throat. 'That was when she decided to tell me about the affair she'd been having with the photographer she's been working with for the last year or two. Nico. They'd broken it off because he was going back to Italy but…he'd asked her to go with him and she'd decided that *was* what she wanted to do. Things went downhill after that and when I asked what about the baby, she said…she said the baby was only mine so I could have it. By myself.'

'Oh, my God…' Alice breathed. Nico's hand was still lying on the table after he'd pushed his cup away and, without thinking, she reached out to put her hand over his. He didn't pull away from her touch. 'I'm so sorry, Nate.'

He was silent for a long moment. Alice felt his hand clench into a fist beneath her fingers.

'I didn't even see it coming,' he said softly. 'She'd seemed so onboard with the plan. We went house-hunting and had an offer accepted on a real family home—a big old villa with a lovely garden.' He closed his eyes, making a sound like a low growl. 'Donna cleared all her stuff out of our apartment and I moved out of it a few days ago. She's on her way to Italy and I'm living in a sea of boxes and a mostly empty house. But, you know what?'

'What?'

'I was coping. Or I thought I was. And I'm sorry I was unpleasant to work with today but I was confident that I wasn't letting the latest disaster derail me enough to interfere with being able to do my job. I should probably have taken a day off to try and sort out the new issue but Aratika is the most solid rock in my life right now. I know people are talking about me at the hospital. Donna still has friends there. I know it's not possible but I have a horrible feeling that the news might reach Simone any day now.'

'What makes you say that?'

'I got an email from Simone this morning. She wants photos of the new house so she can daydream about where the baby is going to grow up.' He pulled his hand away from Alice's. 'It hit me like a brick.'

'Why?'

'Because, when she finds out that I'm going to be a single father, she might decide she's going to keep the baby—which, legally, she's perfectly entitled to do.'

'But she knows you. She knows how much you want this baby and if she hasn't worked out what an amazing father you'll be, *I'll* tell her. I've seen you around babies and kids enough to know that and... I can be very persuasive.' Alice attempted a reassuring smile but she knew it was falling flat.

'She only needs to see the house with nothing but boxes in it to know that I'm not exactly coping.'

'So we'll make it look like you are.' Alice's smile was more confident this time. 'That's something I *can* help with. You wait and see. We'll turn it into the perfect family home for those photos.'

# CHAPTER THREE

WHAT A DIFFERENCE a day could make!

Alice hadn't expected to see Nate waiting for the first patient she and her crew partner brought into the emergency department the next day by air ambulance but he was clearly the consultant who was leading the trauma team for this case.

It wasn't the time or place to exchange any kind of personal greeting and Nate was completely focused on the patient being wheeled into the resuscitation area, but Alice could feel the difference with no more than a graze of eye contact and she knew Nate was on top of his game today. He wasn't feeling anything like as pressured or miserable as he had been yesterday.

She also knew that the evening they'd spent together at the Irish pub was largely responsible for him feeling better and…for just a beat, until they brought the stretcher to a halt beside the bed, ready to transfer this patient into the trauma team's care, she let herself feel good that dinner last night had been her idea. That she'd done something nice for a friend whose life was currently going more than a little pear-shaped.

Then Alice took a deep breath as a word from Nate drew the attention of everyone in the room. Some people were simply standing to one side, arms folded over the disposable aprons protecting their scrubs, as they waited to play their parts—like the less senior doctors who were poised to begin a primary survey, the radiographer and technicians. An orthopaedic surgeon and neurosurgeon who'd been summoned on the basis of the information already transmitted were arriving. Another consultant who was at the head of the bed, in charge of the airway, looked up from checking his equipment as Nate spoke and several nurses, who had roles with medications, IVs or as a runner, stopped what they were doing and listened.

All eyes were on Alice as the senior flight paramedic on this crew, and the handover she needed to do had once been one of the most intimidating parts of her job with the intensity of the way this group of highly skilled and very experienced trauma experts was about to listen to every word she said. Along with the patient—a very scared teenager—who was lying on the stretcher, with no idea of what was going to happen next. Alice took just a moment to touch her arm and smile at her reassuringly before she began speaking.

'This is Melissa Williams, fifteen years old. She's had a fall from a horse during a jumping lesson approximately forty-five minutes ago. The fall was witnessed. Both horse and rider fell and it appeared that the full weight of the horse was on Melissa briefly as it rolled. Ground surface was grass and she was wearing both a back protector and a helmet.'

Alice took a breath. It felt like all the other people in this room were a supporting cast. It was Nate she was speaking directly to.

'On arrival, Melissa's GCS was fifteen and she had ten out of ten pelvic and lower lumbar pain which was preventing her moving her legs. She also has tenderness and guarding over her lower abdomen. No obvious signs of limbs fractures and limb baselines normal but slightly reduced in the right leg.'

Alice was speaking rapidly but clearly, trying to get her information across succinctly but not leave anything important out.

'We applied both a pelvic binder due to the mechanism of injury and clinical signs. C-spine immobilisation is due to Melissa's age and the MOI. She has patent IV access and has had fifty micrograms of fentanyl with good effect—pain score now five. Ondansetron given to prevent nausea. Latest vital signs…' Alice glanced down at her glove where she'd scribbled the figures. 'Heart rate one-twenty, blood pressure ninety-eight over sixty, respiration rate twenty-four, SpO2 ninety-nine. No previous medical history of note and no known allergies. Her family have been contacted and her parents are en route.' Finally, Alice let her gaze sweep the whole room. 'Any questions?'

A beat of silence.

'Thanks, Alice.' Nate's tone was crisp but he was smiling at Melissa. 'Don't worry,' he told her. 'We're going to take very good care of you.'

Alice stood back to let the trauma team transfer Melissa to the bed on Nate's count.

'One…two…*three*!'

All the monitoring equipment like electrode connections, blood pressure cuff and the finger clip to measure blood oxygen saturation level were switched on and, moments later, Alice and her crew partner, Jack, were wheeling the stretcher out with all their gear piled on top.

Alice could hear the team swinging into action behind her, a babble of voices and commands, the squeak of trolleys being repositioned and X-ray machinery being readied but she wasn't really aware of the familiar sounds. She was thinking more about what it would have felt like to be Melissa and to have Nate Madden smiling at her like that just before something new and potentially terrifying might be going to happen.

She would have believed him when he said they were going to take very good care of her, she decided.

She would have felt a whole lot safer.

And you couldn't put a price on being able to make a person who was having the worst day of their life feel like that.

Alice didn't get back to The General's emergency department on that shift. She and Jack were dispatched to a car accident but stood down before they got there because first responders hadn't found injuries that were severe enough to warrant the air ambulance resources. They did an interhospital transfer of a pregnant woman in early labour with a high-risk pregnancy due to her congenital heart disease but that took them to the city's maternity hospital. There were no call-outs for the last couple of hours of her shift and Alice was more than ready to head home when her phone pinged to advertise an incoming text.

From Nate.

If you're not too tired, come and see the house when you're on your way home. You might want to see what you signed up for last night.

He'd ended the message with a crying laughing emoji that made Alice smile.

She sent him a 'thumbs up' reaction and he sent through his address.

Dusk was falling when she arrived on the doorstep of a lovely old villa in a suburb on top of one of Wellington's hills. The fading daylight only made the view out over the city and the harbour more fabulous as lights came on like fireflies gathering over the hills and amongst the high-rise buildings of the city centre. One of the big ferries that provided a vital link between the north and south islands of New Zealand was heading for its wharf and the lights of a helicopter heading back to the Aratika Rescue Base could be seen not far behind the ferry.

'Oh, my goodness,' Alice exclaimed. She was grinning. 'You can sit here on the terrace and almost feel like you're still at work.'

'It was the view that we fell in love with,' Nate said. 'And I had no idea it would be even better in the dark. There's always something happening out there.'

*We…*

Alice's smile faltered at the reminder that Nate and his wife had chosen this house together. It was a symbol of the future as the home where they would raise their baby. The enormity of what had already been taken away from him—even without the unthinkable prospect of being denied his child—was sobering. Alice made an effort to think of something positive to say.

'You've got a straight run into the city and all the drama of this amazing view but, when you walk out of the front door, you've got a lovely, leafy suburb and probably a really good school nearby. It really is the perfect family home. Simone's going to be so impressed.'

'Mmm…' Nate's tone was dubious. 'You mean you didn't notice the "warehouse chic" vibe of all those boxes in the kitchen you just walked straight past?'

'Sorry. This view just sucked me in. I'm ready to appreciate all the character now. I absolutely adore old houses. I live in a little heritage cottage in Aro Valley, so this feels like a palace in comparison. Give me the grand tour and then we'll make a plan for how we're going to stage the photo shoot.'

'Follow me.'

Nate had only unpacked the absolute essentials after the movers had done their job last week. A kettle and a toaster sat on the kitchen bench beside a loaf of bread and a jar of coffee. The pantry shelves were empty and boxes labelled 'kitchen' covered the dining table and were stacked high enough to be hiding the chairs.

'I love that they've kept this old coal range,' Alice said. She bent to trace the decorative markings on the cast-iron appliance next to the fridge.

'It still goes,' Nate told her. 'It burns wood as well as coal.'

He was watching her fingers move over the lettering of the manufacturer's name. He'd seen her hands in action countless times, deftly inserting a cannula into a tricky vein, gently examining a break in a bone or slipping a tube into a difficult airway with an ease that only came with practised skill. Alice didn't wear rings and she kept her nails short and unpainted. They were practical, clever, reliable sort of fingers. How come he'd never noticed that they were also so graceful and…expressive? He could almost feel the appreciation that Alice had for this antique cooker.

It was a weird thing to notice. Nate cleared his throat. 'The previous owners used it for heating and cooking. Might be useful in a power cut.'

'It might.' Alice straightened and her gaze went to the bench. 'Are you living on toast and coffee?' she asked.

'Only for breakfast. I get takeaways when I'm home for dinner.'

'Healthy.'

'I've got some wine in the fridge if you'd like a glass.'

'Maybe later.' Alice was heading for the hallway. 'We've got work to do.'

Nate led her through the house and back down the classic central hallway that was a feature of old villas, with their polished wooden floors and a plaster archway halfway down. The rooms on this upper level of the house were big, with high studs, ornate plaster cornices and central roses on the ceilings, and carved wooden fire surrounds. The staircase led down to bedrooms and bathrooms that looked out onto terraced gardens cut into the hillside. The rumpled linen on his bed and all the clothes still waiting to be hung up that were draped over the end of it were a bit embarrassing but Alice didn't seem to notice. She was captured by the part of the garden that could be seen through this window—a space that was entirely filled with a massive, very old pohutukawa tree.

'*Oh…*' Her face lit up with a smile. 'How gorgeous is that going to be when it's in full flower in December?'

The room she really fell in love with, however, was much smaller than the master bedroom. On the other side of the house, with a small lawn outside the window.

'There's a *Wendy* house,' she exclaimed.

'It was left with the property,' Nate said. 'Because they commissioned it to be a miniature villa and painted it to match the house.'

Donna had seemed just as enchanted by the cute playhouse, with its child-sized front door, but she gave no sign of having had the glimpse of a small person enjoying a tea party or making mud-pies on the tiny porch that had squeezed his own heart so hard. For Nate, that had been the moment he'd really fallen in love with this house.

'This has to be the nursery,' Alice said. 'I can see the photo. A cot here, in the corner by the window with a lovely mobile hanging over it, some cute stuffies on the windowsill and the view into the garden with the Wendy house like a peep into the future when they're big enough to go and play in it.'

Alice seemed a bit startled by the way Nate turned his head so suddenly to stare at her.

'What did I say?'

'Nothing…' Nate tried to find a smile but, strangely, it didn't happen. He also found himself holding eye contact with Alice for just a beat too long.

She was the one who broke it, biting her lip as she turned her gaze back to the window. 'You don't like that idea?'

'Oh, I *do*. It sounds perfect.'

He couldn't tell her how much he really liked it, though. Or why. Maybe he didn't want to think about it too much himself, in fact. It wasn't that it was just the kind of picture he needed to send Simone as proof of how much the baby she was carrying was wanted and would be loved. It was more that imagining a happy child playing in the little house had been the first thought Alice had had. It felt like something had reached between them, on a very personal level, and made contact.

It felt like a secret smile.

Nate turned. It was a welcome distraction to move and head back upstairs.

'We should start making a list of things you need to buy.' Alice was following him. 'We can probably order it online but that might be slower. How much time have we got to make the house look like a baby-friendly home?'

'I told Simone I'd try and send some photos in a few days, as soon as we've tidied up a bit from the move. I guess I could spin that out to a week without her starting to think that anything's really wrong.'

They'd got back to the kitchen now. Nate opened the fridge and held up the bottle of white wine he had chilled.

'Just a small one,' Alice said.

'I'll see if I can unearth a couple of chairs,' Nate said, as he handed her a glass.

He shifted boxes and lifted out chairs which he put in front of the big windows and that view.

'Cheers.'

Alice echoed the toast and they clinked their glasses but neither took their eyes off the view for a moment longer than necessary. It was dark outside and the lights of the city and the moving traffic were even brighter. Even the big Interislander ferry was lit up like a Christmas tree as all the vehicles and passengers were unloaded.

'Why would Simone start thinking anything's wrong?' Alice asked. 'How often does she expect to hear from you?' Her eyes widened. 'Is Donna still in touch with her? Will she have told Simone what's going on?'

Nate shook his head. 'I'm the one who's kept up all the contact since the conception and I sign emails or messages from both of us. Simone talked to Donna a lot during all the calls we made in the early stages of getting to know each other but not lately. I've told her she's out of the country at the moment which is why I'm being slow getting the house sorted. She hasn't asked why Donna's away but I'm guessing she's assuming it's for a work thing, like a photoshoot somewhere exotic. She's probably got used to not talking to Donna now.' His face twisted into a grimace. 'She's never actually met her.'

Alice's glass stopped halfway to her mouth. 'Sorry…*what*?' She put the glass down on the windowsill in front of her. 'How can she be carrying your baby without having met the person who's going to be the mother?'

'I know. It's not exactly usual but everything's been a little…different, I guess. This is a very private arrangement. Simone and her partner live an alternative kind of lifestyle. They're relaxed about time frames and not at all bothered by having patchy internet access. I went down to Dunedin, which is the nearest fertility centre for them, for what was supposed to be the joint counselling session for all four of us involved, but Donna got sick the morning we were due to fly out. It was too late to cancel and we couldn't ask Simone to reschedule at such late notice because they were already in Dunedin and a six-hour drive each way with a car full of kids is such a big deal. Donna managed to join us for a voice call and the meeting went so well that we all agreed that we wanted to move forward without any delays. I did everything I needed to do so that the embryo could be created with the donor egg and Simone signed up to get ready for the first implantation.'

'How long ago was that?'

'A bit over six months. Simone's about nineteen weeks now. Almost halfway. She…' Nate had to stop and clear his throat. 'It wasn't obvious on the first ultrasound but she's convinced she's carrying a girl. She's waiting for an appointment to be confirmed for the anatomy scan, probably the week after next. If I can, I'll go down to Dunedin and be there but how I'm going to explain Donna not coming with me might well be a problem.'

He needed a long sip of his wine as those words hung in the air.

'I don't feel good,' he said then. 'Lying to her, even if it's by omission, like not telling her the real reason Donna's out of the country at the moment. Pretending that nothing's changed and everything's okay feels wrong, too, but…'

Could he tell Alice the real truth? Would she think less of him if he did?

He didn't want Alice to think less of him.

'But you're scared to tell her the truth.' Her voice was very quiet. 'Because she might feel that having a mother is a non-negotiable part of being a family?'

Nate didn't need to say anything. He knew that the moment of meeting Alice's gaze was enough. That feeling of contact was there again. That bond that was on such a personal level it was disconcerting. It didn't feel like a smile this time, though. It was more like an imaginary hand hold. She wasn't judging him for not sharing with Simone all the details of the personal problems he was navigating in his life.

She was in his corner and knowing that was enough to give him a bit of a lump in his throat, to be honest. He wanted her to know how much he appreciated her acceptance of how he was handling this. And he wanted her to know just how important this was for him.

'From the moment I knew I was going to be a father,' he confessed softly, 'I've felt so protective of this baby. Losing the chance to be a part of his—or her—life would haunt me for the rest of *my* life.'

He closed his eyes for a heartbeat. The crazy thought that he could beg Donna to come back for just long enough for the adoption to go through got pushed out of his head as fast as it had appeared.

It did leave a realisation in its wake, however. His marriage *was* over. Deep down, he'd known that for a long time. He just hadn't wanted to admit his failure.

He opened his eyes again. 'I have to tell Simone the truth,' he said. 'But…is it a terrible thing to do to wait a little longer? Long enough to buy some time to try and show her how serious I am about being the best father I can possibly be?'

The short silence that fell created a tension in the air that Nate could almost taste.

'I don't think so,' Alice said then. 'So much has happened and sometimes you need some time to clear your head. How confident you feel about being able to cope as a single dad might make all the difference to how Simone reacts to the news. Taking the first step of getting this lovely home ready for a family won't take that long and you might find it makes a big difference for *you*. It's worth a try, isn't it?'

Nate let his breath out slowly, feeling the tension around him dissipate. There was relief to be found in the prospect of shelving something, albeit temporarily, that could have unpleasant life-changing consequences. It felt like a switch had been flicked and his body was being flooded with a flush of endorphins.

Nate hadn't felt this good in weeks.

Relieved.

Hopeful. Excited, even. With Alice to help, he might be able to get control and start piecing his life back together again.

And yeah…he could add gratitude to the emotions that were making him feel so good.

'Are you hungry?' he asked. 'We could get some food delivered. I might even be able to find a plate or two in one of those boxes.' He waved at the cardboard walls around them. 'Or we could order something that comes in a little box with some wooden chopsticks.'

Alice was laughing. Nate shook his head.

'Okay, okay… I get it. You're *always* hungry.' He was laughing now, too, and it added another boost to the lift in his mood. He liked that Alice made no secret of enjoying her food. He wasn't going to miss watching Donna pick at meals and count every calorie she was consuming. 'What's your favourite to get delivered?'

'Hamburgers,' she said, without hesitation. 'Or pizza. Wait…maybe Mexican?'

Nate pulled out his phone. 'Anything we can eat without cutlery is probably wise.'

But Alice was shaking her head now. 'You order. And then we're going to start unpacking boxes. We might even find your plates and cutlery by the time it's delivered.'

The gourmet hamburgers and hand-cut fries arrived about forty-five minutes later. They had not only found all the plates and cutlery but they were stacked and sorted into cupboards and drawers. They didn't bother using anything that was going to need washing, however. They didn't even sit at the space they'd cleared on the table.

They sat and watched the panorama of lights in the city instead, eating their hamburgers with their hands, the box of chips on the windowsill between their wine glasses.

It felt like a picnic.

'Someone's taking off from Aratika,' Alice observed. 'I used to love being on the night shift crew.' She reached for another chip and dipped it in the little pot of garlic aioli. 'Using night vision goggles is cool and a winch job using the night sun is an incredible adrenaline rush.'

'I've never done a night shift on the base,' Nate said.

'Try one,' Alice suggested. 'As extra crew, maybe.' She smiled. 'Maybe sooner rather than later? You won't be putting your hand up to work at night after your baby arrives. You'll be doing night feeds and watching all the action out of this window instead.'

She made it sound as if there was no doubt that his baby was going to arrive and live here in this house. That he was somehow going to step seamlessly into his new life as a father.

Her confidence was contagious. Nate stuffed the last bite of his burger into his mouth. There were more boxes to unpack. More sorting of his life to get on with and a limited time in which to get it done.

The clock was ticking.

# CHAPTER FOUR

THERE WAS ALWAYS a buzz around shift change-overs, and they were favourite times of the day for Alice, with all the promise of unexpected challenges around the next corner in the morning and the satisfaction of doing her job to the best of her ability at the end of a working day.

The Aratika Rescue Base was humming as dawn broke, as usual, with the night shift clearing up any last-minute tasks to get home and others preparing for the day ahead. There were flight crews, pilots and aircraft engineers along with an ambulance road crew and motorbike paramedics that were positioned on base to back up or complement the city's land-based emergency services. The operations manager, clinical team leader, and communications officer were there and, as often as not, there could also be observers, volunteers or trainees there as well.

There was a loud hum of conversation, greetings being called and the occasional burst of laughter. The atmosphere had the feeling of a tight-knit work community and, judging by the smile on the face of the base's most loyal volunteer, this was Shirley's favourite time of day. She was ruling the kitchen, handing out coffees and bacon rolls, unashamedly eavesdropping on reports of night missions and waiting to hear the briefing Don, the operations manager, would be giving the day shift crews that included any potential issues with equipment, staffing, events happening or weather conditions.

'Thanks, Shirley.' Alice happily accepted a bread roll stuffed with crispy bacon and a drizzle of smoky barbecue sauce. She already had a steaming mug of coffee in front of her at the long table in the mess-room. Don was at the head of the table chatting to departing night shift personnel, a sheaf of papers in his hand ready for his briefing.

'Even my mother didn't look after me as well as you do, Shirley.' Nate also scored one of the hot rolls as he slipped into the empty seat opposite Alice. 'This is exactly what I need to get my engine running this morning.'

'You do look a tad tired, love.' Shirley shook her head, her face creased with the unspoken sympathy of knowing that he was still navigating a major life change. 'I'll get you a coffee.'

Nate's gaze caught Alice's as he took an appreciative bite of his roll and gave her a ghost of a wink. She simply held up her own breakfast, like a toast with a glass, and took a bite herself. She knew exactly why he was tired this morning—they hadn't finished organising his kitchen until midnight last night—but there was no reason for anyone else to know about this new out-of-hours arrangement they had. Alice was smiling inwardly as she remembered how satisfying it had been to admire the neat cupboards and pantry and arrange the chairs around a dining table that was now ready to be used for its intended purpose. And how much fun had it been to squash the empty boxes, jumping on them like a couple of over-excited kids? She hadn't laughed that much in a long time.

It was kind of fun to have a secret with Nate, too.

Alice found her gaze straying back to him more than once as Don got on with an update.

'Weather's great to start the day,' he said. 'Light southerly, ten to fifteen kilometres an hour, temperature getting up to nineteen degrees Celsius and just scattered high cloud. Could be a front moving in later this afternoon, though, with deteriorating conditions.'

Alice wasn't thinking about the weather. Andy would be all over it from a pilot's perspective and she would cope with whatever came their way. For some reason, she was more interested in watching Nate take the last bite of his roll.

He did look tired, she thought. He had a bit of a shadow on his jaw and he hadn't had a haircut for long enough to be revealing waves she didn't know he had. It wasn't a bad look, though. If anything, having a slightly dishevelled vibe made him look even better.

Nate Madden was definitely good-looking, there was no doubt about that. Especially when he was dressed in the standard, indoor, Aratika uniform of black technical pants, steel-capped boots and a black T-shirt with their logo below the left shoulder—the outline of a helicopter flying straight towards a mountain range. Alice had taken a second glance herself, when she'd been first introduced to the new HEMS doctor but she'd already seen his CV and knew he was married, so her appreciation of Nate's looks had never been anything more than purely academic.

Until now…?

Oh, my…

Alice had shifted her gaze at precisely the time Nate was licking a dribble of sauce off his thumb, and her awareness of him was so sharp she could feel it in her body. Deep in her belly. Like…

*No…* Alice might not have felt that particular sensation in a long time but she knew exactly what it was.

Attraction. *Sexual* attraction.

Hastily, she turned her head to focus on Don, but he'd finished what he wanted to say about any current issues being dealt with by other emergency services.

'Have a great day, everyone. And stay safe out there.'

Alice picked up her empty mug. There were plenty of things she needed to get on with before they got their first call-out. She'd already done a check of all the medical packs and the batteries on the defibrillator and portable ventilator, but the drug kit still needed double-checking and she hadn't had time to look at their blood and plasma supplies yet.

She could check all her own gear like her helmet, flight suit and harness. She could even clean her boots if she needed something else to keep her busy. Anything would do, as long as she didn't allow herself to have any more totally inappropriate thoughts or feelings towards her crewmate for the day.

Alice gave herself a mental slap. The man's marriage had only disintegrated five minutes ago, for heaven's sake. And Nate was about to become a father in the near future! Even if he'd been single for a decade, that would be enough of a red flag to make sure Alice was not going to think about Nate as anything other than a friend. With no benefits whatsoever on the horizon.

He certainly wouldn't be having any odd reactions to being around her. She'd met Donna briefly at a Christmas social function at the base not long after Nate had joined the team. The fact that they were both brunettes was the only thing she'd had in common with Nate's wife. Donna was taller, a lot slimmer and far more elegant than Alice could ever dream of being. No wonder she'd given up nursing to become a model.

Okay…maybe neither of them wanted to have children but Alice didn't want to find anything else in common with Donna Madden. Maybe you couldn't judge relationships from the outside but she could be quite confident that Nate had been the one who'd put the most effort into trying to make their marriage work. He was the one who'd dreamed of a happy family future and he was the one who was now rattling around in a big house by himself, determined to do whatever it took to keep at least part of that dream alive.

She was most definitely on Team Nate—more than happy to provide practical help and any support he might accept from a friend. On a deeper level, there was a developing closeness that was making her appreciate Nate in areas she hadn't even considered and she was even more impressed with him as a person. Whose heart wouldn't melt over a man who was prepared to do whatever it took to protect his baby? Or who'd fallen in love with a property because of the adorable Wendy house in the garden?

Alice's heart melted a little bit more when she saw Nate taking his empty mug back to the bench and dropping a kiss on Shirley's cheek to thank her for breakfast. Oh, yeah… Team Nate. She was ready to defend him from any gossip or threat that might undermine his ability to achieve that dream.

The project had just graduated from something nice to do for a friend to something that was more than nice to do for herself.

Something important.

A gift. For Nate.

Nate hadn't had a genuinely close friend who was female since he was at primary school.

By the time he started high school, girls were scary and when they weren't, it felt like there was always a sexual undercurrent to friendships. Or hidden barriers because the girls he would have liked to have been friends with were dating someone and that made it unacceptable to spend time with them alone. Study had been more important than anything else at medical school and it wasn't until Nate had started his final year as a trainee intern position at one of New Zealand's largest hospitals that fate had given him a nudge and he'd met Donna on his first rotation.

The nudge was all the more potent because that first run was on the obstetrics and gynaecology ward and there were babies everywhere—a subconscious shove, in fact, to remind him that there was more to life than his chosen career. They'd become engaged the night he graduated from medical school and were married within a few months. And that, inevitably, put even more solid barriers in the way of having a close friendship with another woman.

Work pressures and a focus on their new life as a couple pretty much made friendship with anyone difficult to maintain. They did things with other couples and the relationships were friendly but not that close. Moving cities more than once to find new opportunities for training and then the consultant position Nate had dreamt of made their social life even more insular. In retrospect, it had created pressure that could have been responsible for the cracks in their marriage to widen beyond a point where they could have been repaired.

Nate wasn't oblivious to the subtle change in the way some women were regarding him as the news of his separation spread, but he didn't have the slightest interest in responding to any invitations. What he *had* needed, without realising it, was a close friend. He might have been wary of that friend being a female but he'd been working with Alice for a long time now and she was already in the friend zone.

Maybe it was strange that they could be real friends when they both wanted completely different things from their personal lives, but perhaps that was also what was making it work. Making this a completely *safe* friend zone because here he was about to become a father and Alice had told him that she never wanted to have children. There was no hidden agenda on her part, that was for sure. There was no need to even set boundaries because it was so blatantly obvious that they could never be anything more than friends, but the change that was happening in their relationship had been a turning point for Nate and he was more than grateful it was happening. It was a lifeline, to be honest. He had someone in his corner and it was giving him a new confidence and hope for his immediate future.

Right now, as they pushed the helicopter stretcher, laden with gear, into a small rural medical centre, he was starting to wonder if it was also changing the way they worked together.

The way they had been in sync professionally had been clear from the first mission they'd ever been on together when they'd had a fight on their hands to save a man whose motorbike had been clipped by a concrete mixer truck. Nate had been so impressed with his new partner that he'd told the operations manager that he was looking forward to working with Alice on future shifts. He'd been crewed with Alice so often since then that they had earned the nickname of Aratika's Dream Team but had he ever felt that he and Alice were *this* solid before?

That there wasn't anyone else he would feel this confident with, walking into a situation that could potentially be a matter of life or death?

The look of relief on the GP's face as they were directed into the consulting room advertised what had been an anxious wait for the air ambulance. Their patient, lying back on the pillows of the bed, looked surprisingly cheerful. He was, in fact, grinning at Alice.

'G'day,' he said. 'I'm feeling better already.'

'G'day,' Alice responded. 'I'm Alice and this is Nate.'

'This is Trevor Henley,' the GP said. 'He's seventy-two years old and he was out doing some fencing on the farm this morning when he got acute pain in his lower back, radiating to his legs, that was bad enough to make him feel a bit faint.'

'It's not so bad now,' Trevor declared.

'He looked very unwell when he arrived here,' the GP continued. 'Pale and sweaty, GCS fifteen, pain score six out of ten, but Trev's inclined to downplay symptoms. He's had some morphine and reckons it's down to four now.'

'Two,' Trevor put in. 'I'm almost cured, Doc.'

Nate smiled at him. 'Is it okay if we have a look at you, mate? I'd like to make sure you're okay to come for a ride with us.'

'Do I really need to? That fencing isn't going to do itself and I don't want my sheep getting out on the road.'

'Better safe than sorry.' Alice was smiling at Trevor. 'And it's a lovely morning for a ride in a chopper.' Her tone was persuasive. 'A bit of time off wouldn't hurt, would it?'

'I guess not.' Trevor leaned his head back on the pillows. The anxious lines on his face that belied his casual cheerfulness softened as he let himself accept that he needed help. 'You do whatever you think's best.'

'And you just relax and let us look after you,' Alice said. 'I'm going to take your blood pressure again, okay?' She took out the blood pressure cuff from the pouch on the side of the defibrillator and wrapped it around Trevor's upper arm.

Nate had been about to ask her to take another set of vitals. Instead, he picked up the twelve lead ECG the GP had recorded.

'Trev's got a past history of hypertension,' she told him. 'Mild to moderate COAD from smoking and he started getting a bit of angina a couple of years ago which is stable and relieved by GTN. Do you want a list of his medications?'

'Yes, please.' Nate looked up from the graph recording the electrical activity of the heart. 'Your ticker looks like it's behaving itself, Trevor. That's good news.'

Nate could feel Alice's glance in his direction. She knew why he was sounding so reassuring. They'd been dispatched due to the GP finding a pulsatile abdominal mass, making a provisional diagnosis of an abdominal aortic aneurysm, then doing an ultrasound to find that blood was leaking from a rupture of the major blood vessel.

The last thing they wanted to happen with someone who had a leaking aneurysm was for them to get really anxious, increase their blood pressure and potentially extend a small rupture into something large enough to be very rapidly catastrophic.

'Blood pressure's one-ten on seventy-five,' Alice said, writing it on her glove. 'Heart rate's one-oh-six and SPO2's ninety-four.' She turned back to their patient and put her hand over his. 'Your hands are a bit cold, Trevor.'

'Cold hands, warm heart,' he said.

'Absolutely,' Alice agreed. 'But how 'bout we get you comfy on our stretcher and wrap you up in some of our lovely warm blankets?'

Nate added the information about Trevor's cool

peripheries that Alice had casually given him to the fact that the blood pressure had dropped since arrival at the medical centre and the heart rate was going up—all possibly signs of an increasing internal blood loss.

He liked the way Alice was keeping things so calm. The idea of her tucking someone up in warm blankets was making him feel more relaxed. He saw the squeeze Alice gave Trevor's hand before she let go, as well, and he could almost feel that himself.

Yeah…there was something new in how it felt to be working with her. They'd always been in tune clinically and able to follow a line of thought or anticipate the next intervention that was needed, and Nate knew this change wasn't due to anything professional, but he didn't give it another moment's thought until they had Trevor safely packaged and on board the helicopter with all the monitoring equipment in place and a new, wide-bore IV line in his arm.

Alice was adjusting the drip rate after hanging a bag of fluid as Nate finished securing the line.

'TKVO?' she asked.

Nate nodded. A minimal amount of fluid to keep the vein open was exactly what they needed. Allowing Trevor's blood pressure to stay high enough to maintain perfusion and consciousness but low enough to avoid increasing any bleeding was the goal.

They had a flight time of about twenty minutes to get to the hospital and they needed to monitor Trevor continuously, taking his blood pressure every few minutes and checking heart and respiration rates, peripheral pulses and skin colour. They'd given him a headset to wear so that they could talk to him about any changes in his symptoms but also so that they could explain what was going on and keep him reassured.

'How's that pain, Trevor?' he asked, noticing a grimace. 'Would you like a top-up of the pain meds?'

'Nah… I'm all good.'

'Don't be a hero, Trevor.' Alice leaned closer. She'd also seen the truth in his face. 'We want you to be as comfortable as possible. I've got it right here, if you'd like a drop more.'

'Go on, then…' Trevor managed a smile. 'Just a drop.'

Alice injected the dose of morphine. She leaned forward once she was strapped into her seat and held Trevor's hand as the noise level increased and they lifted off. Nate could see how fiercely he was gripping it back. Alice's fingers looked squashed but she wasn't moving her hand. Instead, she was trying to distract Trevor's attention to lessen his fear.

'What sort of sheep do you run, Trevor? Romneys?'

'Yep.'

'They're the best choice for both meat and wool, aren't they?'

'Yep. How do you know about sheep?'

'I grew up in the country and Romneys are my favourite—they've got nice faces, haven't they? I bottle-raised one. I called her Barbra. My mother's boyfriend at the time insisted on calling her Sunday.'

Trevor seemed to be forgetting how nervous he was and actually chuckled. 'As in Sunday roast?'

'That's the one.' Alice shook her head. 'Barbra went back to the farm eventually but I was quite happy that she lasted longer than that particular boyfriend did.'

Maybe it was the way Alice turned to catch his gaze to see if he was sharing the amusement. Or perhaps it was because he was suddenly curious enough to want to know more about her childhood. What had happened to her father? And had she ended up with a stepfather she approved of? What he was really conscious of, however, was that he could see what was different about his working relationship with Alice Barlow. She was a lot more than simply a colleague now. More than a casual kind of friend whose help he was grateful for.

He really liked her. He'd always known how much he liked working with her, but now he knew he liked her without being anywhere near the environment of a shared career they were both so passionate about. He could enjoy eating dinner with her. Pushing furniture around and jumping on cardboard boxes. Talking to her about things that had nothing to do with medicine was surprisingly easy. So natural that Nate felt like he could tell her anything. He'd already told her far more than anyone else knew about what was going on in his life. Being in her company away from work was…

Welcome, that's what it was. Really, really welcome.

Nate hadn't realised how lonely he'd been in the last weeks. Maybe his marriage hadn't been anything like what he'd hoped it would be, especially in recent years, but he'd never been entirely alone, either. A huge part of his life had been ripped away and left a gap that felt painfully raw. Worse, he'd had to pack up everything left after Donna had taken what she wanted from their apartment and then move from one almost empty dwelling to a new one. It had been lonely, beyond sad and totally exhausting. He'd barely smiled for what felt like far too long but he'd laughed out loud at Alice's reaction to that strong

Guinness she'd tasted for the first time and he'd laughed even more last night, when Alice had insisted they flatten all those boxes before putting them out for recycling.

Alice had been laughing, too. He could remember the joyful sound of it and the way he could feel it as much as hear it. The way bits of her hair had dislodged themselves from her ponytail. The way her eyes were sparkling from the fun of behaving in such a juvenile fashion.

His thoughts, as he listened to Alice keeping Trevor distracted, had been no more than a flash of feeling more than anything as coherent as words but Nate gave himself a mental shake to get rid of them. He needed to be on high alert right now. If Trevor's aneurysm ruptured, he could crash. He might lose consciousness and need a blood transfusion, intubation or full resuscitation from a cardiac arrest. Nate's focus sharpened as he ran through a checklist of everything they might need in a hurry, like rapid sequence intubation drugs and the airway kit.

Banishing any thoughts remotely personal didn't mean they'd entirely evaporated, mind you. Something was left behind. Something nebulous but pleasant, like a waft of a subtle perfume or the memory of a hug from somebody who mattered. He had Alice by his side and that was making the world a better place to be in.

* * *

The drama of flying over the cityscape of New Zealand's capital city and landing on the roof of its biggest hospital never got old for Alice and it was particularly satisfying to have a case with the kind of urgency a triple A generated and get their patient to definitive medical care in time to save his life.

They got Trevor unloaded, into the lift and down to the emergency department without his condition deteriorating any further. A full resus team, including the vascular surgeon on call, was ready for them and after a rapid handover, the switch of monitoring equipment and a repeated assessment, Trevor's bed was wheeled swiftly out of the area, a theatre on standby so that his aneurysm could be repaired.

Alice was coiling electrode wires and slotting them neatly into the side pocket of the defibrillator on top of their stretcher as the doors swung shut behind Trevor's bed. Nate finished the last of the paperwork and handed it to ED staff to file.

'He's a lucky man,' Nate said, taking the front end of the stretcher to help steer it out of the department.

'He sure is,' Alice agreed. 'I was really worried that he was going to crash, especially when I saw how nervous he was about flying.' She kept a hand on the other end of the stretcher as they went down a corridor and then into the busy foyer. The lift that would take them back to the helipad on the hospital's roof was to one side of the main reception desk, just past the gift shop.

Nate steered them to one side, to allow room for a hospital bed to dodge a woman with a pushchair. They were right beside the window of the gift shop and Alice was scanning the usual offerings of hand creams and soaps, fluffy socks, get-well cards and children's toys as they went past. Her tug on the stretcher brought them to a sudden halt and Nate's head swerved.

'What's up?'

'That…' Alice pointed. 'Look…'

She'd never seen anything quite as cute as the honey-coloured, curly-haired rabbit with long, droopy ears but what made it totally irresistible was that it was wearing a doctor's white coat, with a red cross embroidered on the pocket.

Nate looked bemused.

'Wait there. I'll be two ticks.' Alice dived into the shop and came out only moments later, clutching the rabbit. 'This,' she informed Nate, 'is the best possible thing to go on the windowsill of the nursery. It couldn't be more perfect.'

They needed other items for the nursery, of course, and it was a few days before they found the time to visit one of the biggest baby supply shops in town. The larger purchases, like the cot and change table, shelving units and a rocking chair, would be delivered the next day. The back seat and hatch of Nate's SUV was stuffed with everything else. Linen, clothes, nappies, a baby swing, books and toys, and a mobile that was almost as cute as the gift shop rabbit. Small brightly coloured flowers, leaves and bumble bees made of felt were light enough to move in any breeze, and the mobile could be wound up to rotate slowly to the traditional music of 'Brahms' Lullaby.'

They put the whole nursery together the next weekend when their days off coincided and it *did* look perfect. The cot in the corner had the mobile hanging over it, the rocking chair beside the change table had a soft lemon-yellow blanket draped over it and the cube-style shelving was filled with neat stacks of clothing, soft toys and picture books.

Nate pulled his phone out. 'The rest of the house can wait but I've got to send Simone a photo of this right now.'

'Wait!' Alice ran to where she'd left her shoulder bag. 'We're missing Dr Rabbit. He's got to be on the windowsill for the photos.'

But Nate was already taking photos by the time she got back to prop the rabbit on one side of the window.

'There we go,' she said. 'Now it's perfect.'

But Nate was looking at his phone and Alice couldn't interpret his expression. She went and stood beside him and peered at the screen. The image had everything she'd imagined, with the cot and the view through the window to the Wendy house but he'd taken it as she was putting the rabbit down and the blurry shape of her moving figure filled half the screen.

'Take another one,' she suggested. 'Without me ruining it.'

'You're not ruining it,' Nate said quietly. 'Simone's going to think it's Donna.'

Alice gave a huff. 'Are you kidding? Donna's a *model*.'

'It's the colour of your hair,' Nate said. 'And the way it's blurry. It…' He was taking in a slow breath. 'It looks like a mum who can't wait to welcome her baby.' He cleared his throat. 'Would it be okay if I sent this one?'

Alice blinked but then shrugged. 'Sure…why not? It's not as if anyone could recognise me. Or that we were trying to deceive anyone.'

But for the space of time it took to draw in a new breath, it felt like she was trying to deceive herself. Because, for a split second, she could imagine that she *was* the woman Simone would expect to see. Getting a nursery ready for the baby she was going to love and nurture and…

and it felt like a dream. One that would never have occurred to her if it wasn't Nate standing beside her—the man who so passionately wanted a family of his own. It was also one that would be dismissed as soon as she stepped out of this room, of course. It wasn't *her* dream.

It never would be.

Nate tapped on the screen of his phone and then slid the device back into his pocket. 'You're a star,' he told Alice. 'I couldn't have done this without you.'

He was smiling at her. And then, unexpectedly, he was hugging her. Just the kind of swift, squeezy sort of hug that a friend would share when they were grateful for something.

But it didn't quite feel like that.

Alice was too aware of the shape of Nate's body pressed against her own. The way it felt to be inside the circle of his arms. She could feel his warmth and his breath on her hair. She could even feel his heart beating for the beat or two that she was that close to his skin, and it was doing something to her body. Something melty. Something that was making the floor oddly uneven beneath her feet when he let her go.

Maybe Nate could feel it, too?

He was holding her gaze the way she was holding his—as if it was the best anchor to ride out the wobbly floor sensation—but who was going to break it first? Alice could feel it going on that beat too long.

She could see that something else was forming in that space of time. Another nanosecond and she knew that Nate would be kissing her.

Or she'd be kissing him.

However it happened, there would be no coming back from it. And what quicker way could there be to ruin a friendship?

Suddenly, it was easy to break the eye contact. Perhaps because they'd both done it—and stepped back—in the same instant?

Thank goodness it seemed to be just as easy to pretend it had never happened.

And maybe that was because it was what they both desperately wanted to believe?

# CHAPTER FIVE

'WHAT DID SHE SAY?'

Alice kept her voice down but the noise level in a very busy emergency department was more than enough to cover having a private word with Nate, who was staring at an X-ray image on a wall screen. They both had their backs to the usual hum of staff and patients moving, trolleys and machines being wheeled from one place to the next, and a cleaner trying to mop up what looked like a bloodstain on the floor.

Alice held up her hand to signal her crew partner who was still moving their stretcher towards the doors. Jack nodded. He knew she would catch up with him by the time he got to the lift.

'Did she love the Wendy house?' she asked. 'And the doctor bunny?'

Nate shrugged. 'She hasn't responded. Could be that the text message didn't get through because it was a picture. I'll email it when I get a minute.' Nate's gaze swept around the busy emergency department. 'But I don't think Simone checks her emails every day, either.'

'She'll love it, don't worry.'

But, even though Alice only saw Nate from a distance the next day, it was obvious that he still hadn't had any contact. She could see it in his body language. When he looked up and saw that she was in the department, just a heartbeat of eye contact made her realise she could actually feel that he wasn't happy—as if his mood was something invisible but tangible in the air—as obvious as the smell of the disinfectant often was around here.

And that was when Alice started to wonder if something was amiss. She called Nate that evening.

'She gave the picture a "thumbs up" reaction but didn't say anything. Not a word.'

'At least she likes it.'

'It just feels like she doesn't want to talk to me for some reason. I'm wondering if Donna's been in touch with her and she knows what's going on and she's trying to decide what to do about it.'

'She might just be busy. Didn't you say she's got *five* kids? That would make anybody's life hectic.'

'That's true. And she'll have some organising to do so that she can get up to Dunedin for the day and have the anatomy scan. She's never been great with communication, either. They only need a bit of bad weather to lose their internet connection. Or get a power cut. Maybe her phone's dead.'

'Has she got an appointment for the scan?'

'Yes. End of this week. Friday.'

'Are you going down?'

'I'm wait-listed for a seat—there's a big rugby game on that weekend and everything's booked out at the moment. If I can't make it, Simone's going to get a video of the scan and then she'll ring me as soon as she can.'

'There you go, then. Not long to wait.'

The silence told her that it felt like a long time to Nate.

'Why don't you send her another picture? Of the garden or the rest of the house?'

'I did think of that. I wandered around looking for something that looked…' His voice trailed off as if he hadn't actually been too sure of what he was looking for.

'Something homely?' Alice suggested. 'Like a happy parent-to-be is living there?'

'Yeah…and the only room that looks like that is the nursery. Everything else is a bit…empty? As if nobody's *really* living here. Maybe I need to hang up some pictures.'

'That would be a good start. And you could fill the bookshelves. Books always make rooms look like home. Put some photos around, too. A fruit bowl on the dining table? And knick-knacks.'

'Knick-knacks?' Nate sounded bemused.

'You know...things like souvenirs or small sculptures or bowls. Vases. Antique bottles or jars. Candlesticks. Pretty things or personal stuff.'

'I think Donna took most of that kind of stuff. And the only books I've kept are textbooks. That built-in bookshelf in the living room is completely empty.'

'That's an easy fix,' Alice assured him. 'We could hit the second-hand shops. Are you working tomorrow?'

'I've swapped to cover someone for the last half of a swing shift—5 p.m. till midnight. He got invited last minute to a stag do and has promised to cover a full shift for me sometime in return for the favour.'

'Excellent. I've got a day off. Let's go and do some power shopping. There are some great antique shops in the central city and I just happen to know the best second-hand bookshop in town.'

Nate had expected their mission to add to the tension of not knowing what was going on in Simone's head but, in fact, it did the opposite.

Not just by being enough of a distraction.

Or even that it was far more fun than he expected it to be.

It almost felt like he was travelling back in time. Reminding himself of long-forgotten parts of his life and, even better, sharing them with someone who was genuinely interested.

They started in a huge, second-hand bookshop where he recognised the covers and titles of books from the days before he began to study so hard. When he could banish any loneliness that came from being an only child by escaping into other worlds and the company of fictional friends and enthralling adventures.

He picked up a set of Tolkien books.

'My dad read me *The Hobbit* as a bedtime story when I was about seven years old,' he told Alice. 'I had nightmares about giant spiders and dragons but that didn't stop me going back to read it for myself a couple of years later.'

'Scary stuff is kind of delicious when you know it's safe.' Alice was smiling. 'If it gets really bad you know you can just shut the book.'

'Oh, I knew it was safe. It was my dad reading it to me and he was my absolute hero. I would have felt safe if it had been *real* dragons in my bedroom as long as he was there with me.' Nate was smiling. The sadness had become muted over the years but it would always be there in the background.

The look Alice gave him made him wonder

if she could hear more than what he was saying in his voice.

'What did your dad do?' she asked.

'He was a firefighter. A real-life hero.'

Yeah… Alice knew that this was breaking off a little bit of his heart. How astonishingly perceptive was this woman? And how sensitive. She wasn't about to pry into something he might not want to share. Except he did. There was something about Alice that made him feel, in some ways, almost as safe as he had with his dad.

'He died on the job,' Nate added quietly. 'A warehouse fire where the roof collapsed without warning.'

'How old were you?'

'Fourteen. Old enough to know I needed to step up and look after my mum. Young enough to be totally lost without my dad. It wasn't just that he made me feel so safe. The best feeling in the world was when he was proud of me. It…' He eyed Alice. 'This is going to sound daft but it made me feel like I could do anything as long as he was there to watch. Fly, even…'

Alice's smile was softer than he'd ever seen before. 'It's not daft,' she said. 'How lucky were you to have a dad like that?'

Nate nodded. It was time to change the subject before that lump in his throat got any bigger. He found a smile.

'It's why I've always wanted to be a dad myself,' he told her. 'To be able to make my own kids feel like that. I reckon that would have made my dad the proudest he'd ever been.'

'You need this book,' she said, taking the slightly tattered old version of the beloved story from his hands. 'It might be a while before you're going to be reading it aloud but it'll be good to have it handy.'

She added it to the box on the floor that was already full of the science fiction and mystery books that had also been favourites.

'I'm going to get another box,' she said. 'You need some chick lit on the shelves as well. Oh… and recipe books for the kitchen.'

They went to a coffee shop for morning tea after loading the boxes of books into Nate's car and then to a massive antique shop, with room after room of everything from total junk to priceless collectibles.

Alice found an old crystal vase. He found a huge yellow ceramic bowl that was hand-painted with the leaves, flowers and fruit of a strawberry patch.

'My grandma had one just like this,' he said in amazement.

'Good find.' Alice nodded. 'Everybody has a couple of precious things they've inherited in their houses.'

'And look at these…' Nate peered into a glass cabinet that was stuffed with Matchbox cars a few minutes later. 'I had some when I was a kid. Might still have a couple buried in a box in my parents' garage.'

'Buy some more,' Alice said. 'You can add yours later. They'd look perfect on the top of a bookshelf or the mantelpiece in the living room.' She was smiling at him. 'I can just see you playing with cars when you were a wee boy. Making roads in the dirt or the sandpit. You would have been so cute.'

Nate smiled back. He liked that Alice thought he might have been a cute kid. He liked that she was interested in his childhood. He was, he realised suddenly, very interested in hers.

'What did *you* play with?' he asked. 'Dolls?'

Alice made a face as she shook her head. 'I had a doll,' she said. 'A very realistic baby one. I gave it to the girl who lived down the street.'

'Wow…' Nate blinked as he remembered something that Alice had said that night at the Irish pub.

*I thought the one thing that would make life perfect was not to have a family at all…*

'You started early, didn't you?' he asked quietly. 'Not wanting kids?'

Alice nodded. She had turned away to look at a display of antique cast-iron pots and pans.

'My mother got pregnant when she was nineteen,' she said, glancing over her shoulder at Nate. 'And her boyfriend refused to be involved. So there she was, in her twenties, stuck at home with a baby, when all her old friends were out having fun, going to uni, starting jobs and finding relationships. By the time I was four or five, I knew that it was my fault that she was never going to find a husband. Never going to be happy. That was about the time I decided I never wanted to be a mother and I gave the doll away.' She shrugged. 'Don't you think these pots and pans would be fabulous hanging over the old coal range?'

She was changing the subject but that didn't stop Nate continuing to think about Alice as a small girl.

That she'd been made to feel unwanted was heartbreaking.

He picked up a pair of rather tarnished silver candlesticks that still had half-burned candles in them but turned his head towards Alice again.

'Did she find what she wanted? Did things get better for your mum?'

'She kept trying,' Alice said. 'But nothing lasted, even when I was old enough to not be in the way so much. She died when I was thirteen. She stepped off a footpath and got hit by a bus and...that was that. She was gone. I got sent off to live with my grandmother in a small town up north. Neither of us was that thrilled about it.'

Nate was staring at her. Had her mother's death been an accident? Had her grandmother also made her feel like she was in the way? He didn't feel like he could ask such personal questions, especially not in public, but he couldn't blame Alice for still believing that having a family wasn't the road to happiness. What else had she told him that night? That she'd found men who said they didn't want to have kids but they were just filling in time until they found the women who *did* want to have their babies?

It was probably just as well that Alice was looking at the candlesticks and didn't see the sympathy that had to be written all over his face.

'Good choice,' she said. 'Put it on the dining table and it'll look as though you and Donna make a habit of romantic dinners. Simone will notice that in the photos.'

Nate said very little as they walked back to the car with their purchases. It wasn't just that he'd found the glimpse into Alice's childhood sobering. Her comment about the candlesticks had made him realise he couldn't remember the last time he'd felt the magic of real romance.

Maybe he'd never find it again but he could live with that. At least he'd know he was safe.

That was when he felt a solid beat of something much stronger than sympathy for Alice. He understood why she'd built walls around the very idea of having a family of her own. She was simply trying to keep herself safe. To protect her heart.

He got that.

The recent setbacks he'd encountered were far less than Alice had dealt with in her life, but it still felt like a real bond between them. That Alice chose that moment to create a physical bond by putting her hand on his arm to stop him walking felt like more than a coincidence.

They were in front of a modern homewares store.

'Look at that.' Alice was pointing at a framed picture of a row of old silver spoons overflowing with vibrant spices like saffron and paprika and pink peppercorns.

'You need that,' she declared. 'In the kitchen. It would look fabulous in that gap between the fridge and the door into the living room.'

Nate was staring at the picture but all he could think about was the feeling of Alice's hand on his arm.

'You could put a wine rack underneath it. I'll bet they sell wine racks in here, too. Come on…' Her hand slid down his arm and grabbed his hand to pull him towards the doors of the shop.

She let go as soon as she was happy that he was following her, and Nate tried to brush off the memory of the touch. The way he'd brushed off that odd moment in the nursery the other day—after he'd hugged her as an impetuous way of thanking her for helping him bring the fantasy of his child's bedroom to life.

The moment when he'd thought about kissing her? A tiny flick of time when kissing her was the one thing he really *wanted* to do?

The last thing Nate wanted was for this lifeline of a friendship to get ruined by the kind of sexual undercurrents that always made things turn awkward when only one person was having those thoughts. The eye contact had been broken so decisively that he'd known it had only been wishful thinking that he'd seen what looked like a reflection of his own, errant desire in *her* eyes.

He didn't need to try and read anything into being touched on the arm, either. Not when Alice was clearly intent on something else. She'd asked a shop assistant if they had wine racks available and, on the way, had picked up a big bunch of brightly coloured artificial flowers.

'For that crystal vase,' she said with satisfaction. 'We'd better stop after this so you've got time to put things where they belong before you have to get to work. Send me some photos later?'

* * *

A photo pinged into Alice's phone when she was sitting in her small apartment that evening looking at the mess she'd made after she got home, inspired to sort out some of the clutter stuffed into the cupboard under the stairs.

The first photo was simply the silver candlesticks on Nate's dining table on either side of the antique bowl which was unexpectedly filled with an array of fresh fruit. Bananas, red apples, oranges and kiwifruit. Beyond the colourful display, Alice could see the blurry twinkle of city lights through the window and it reminded her of sitting there with Nate eating burgers. After she'd agreed that it wouldn't be a bad thing to cover up what was going on in his personal life long enough to give the impression that, even though he was going to be a single father, he was going to have his life completely under control.

With the speed of light, that memory morphed into standing in the newly furnished nursery and the feeling of Nate's arms around her as he gave her a hug and seeing that look in his eyes, yet again, with a clarity that didn't show any signs of diminishing. If anything, it was sharper. She could feel the points of it digging into some deep places in her body and it felt very much like…

Lust. If she was honest with herself, the more she thought about that moment, the more enticing the thought of kissing Nathaniel Madden was becoming.

She actually shook her head to dislodge the thought, her thumbs busy responding to the message.

Looks great. Did you get the pots hung up?

No. I need to go to the hardware shop for some hooks.

That felt like the end of the conversation. Nate was probably busy with a constant flow of patients in the emergency department, so Alice opened the box she'd dragged out of the cupboard. It was full of half-finished craft projects like a jumper she'd started knitting last year, cross-stitch patterns and some very dried-up oil paints and brushes from even longer ago when a paint-by-numbers project seemed like a nice hobby for winding down after work. She was taking the paints and small canvas to the rubbish when her phone pinged again.

Alice enlarged the picture so she could see what Nate had done with all the sections of the built-in shelves in the living room beside the fireplace, smiling at the instant effect that books could have to make a room look lived in and friendly. The vase full of pretty artificial flowers was on one corner of the top shelf and, beside it, the collection of tiny cars and trucks were lined up. Her smile widened. She could imagine Nate arranging them.

She could almost see him as a small boy, playing with his own small cars. In a room by himself because he didn't have the siblings he'd wanted so much for company, and it squeezed her heart. Hard.

Good job, she messaged back. Love the cars and the flowers. I think you need some pot plants in the house, too. I can go and choose a couple, if you like.

Please. I wouldn't have a clue about pot plants.

I'm off on Friday. I'll go to the garden centre and drop them off on your doorstep.

Might be here myself, waiting for a call from Simone. Haven't got a ticket yet and they're not putting on any more flights.

What time is the scan?

First thing in the morning. But she didn't say what time she'd ring and I don't want to pester her.

Alice went back to the box and started sorting all the balls of wool that were getting tangled up. She was still thinking about Nate. She knew that the anatomy scan was a big deal. It was a milestone in any pregnancy and it was a long and possibly tense appointment if someone was worried about potential complications like a low-lying placenta for the mother or issues like congenital heart defects for the baby. Would being so far away make it harder for Nate to wait for the results? Maybe he'd be bursting to tell her all about it when she arrived with those pot plants, because she was the only one he could tell, wasn't she? The only one who knew his secret.

Alice was smiling again. She was about to throw the ball of wool she'd rewound back into the box but, instead, she stared at it thoughtfully. It was lovely and soft in a pale shade of yellow. Somewhere in this box, she was sure she had a book of patterns for baby clothes, like little hats and bootees. She kept the wool out and began searching for a pair of needles. Baby stuff was so quick to make and what better way to spend an evening by herself than by finding a good movie and knitting?

*Really?*

Good grief... Had her personal life shrunk enough that having the kind of evening an elderly woman might enjoy was appealing?

Alice found herself picking up her phone. Reading Nate's texts again.

If he couldn't get on a flight he'd be home on Friday morning when she dropped off those plants. Would he want some company if he was stressing about the phone call he'd be waiting for?

Would he want *her* company?

Would she *want* him to want her company?

Judging by the way her heart rate had picked up noticeably as she'd been scanning those messages and that any desire to start knitting had completely evaporated, the answer to that question was more than obvious.

*Yes…*

# CHAPTER SIX

DESPITE BEING AT the airport ready to take advantage of any no-shows for the early flights to Dunedin that Friday morning, Nate was more than disappointed to find himself out of luck. Passing a hardware store on his way home from the airport gave him the distraction that he knew he was going to need. Getting stuck into the final touches his new home was begging for was as good a way as any to fill in a long morning, waiting for a call he was probably not going to get before lunchtime.

He put up hooks to hang the antique pots and pans in the alcove above the old coal range and put the copper kettle on a hotplate beneath them. Then he hung the picture of the spice spoons in exactly the spot Alice had thought it would work. Having positioned the elegant wrought iron wine rack beneath it, he stood back to admire the effect and found he was nodding in admiration. He'd have to tell her that she had a real gift for interior design the next time he saw her.

As if he'd somehow made it happen, the doorbell rang and he found Alice standing outside, with pot plants in her arms and a larger one at her feet. She must have been unloading her car while he had been standing there admiring the new additions to his kitchen. This was an even better distraction than the handyman tasks he'd been keeping busy with and he knew he had a stupidly wide smile on his face. He hadn't intended sharing what was going through his head but it came out anyway.

'I was just thinking about you,' he said. 'And here you are.'

'Were you?' Alice was smiling, too. 'And yes, here I am. Bearing plants. I thought you'd be in Dunedin by now, though.'

'No such luck. I missed out on getting a seat.' Nate dropped his gaze from where it seemed to have caught on her smile. 'That plant's more like a tree!'

'It is. It's a fig tree. I thought it would look great in that empty corner of the living room beside the bay window. Can you carry it? My hands are kind of full.'

'Of course.'

Alice put the plants down on the kitchen bench. 'The little pots of herbs are for the windowsill here and this fern can hang in a bathroom, perhaps.' She took off her coat and draped it over the back of a chair, along with her shoulder bag. 'There was a café in the garden centre so I got some sandwiches because I was really hungry.'

Nate was on his way into the living room with the largest pot. 'Is there any time when you're *not* really hungry?' he called over his shoulder.

Alice didn't respond. When Nate put the tree in its place and went back, he found her taking in the artwork and wine rack and the accessories for the coal range.

'This looks *amazing*,' she said. But her smile faded a little as she held his gaze. 'Has Simone called yet?'

'No.'

'She will. Probably by the time we've had some lunch.' She produced paper bags with freshly made sandwiches in them. 'Ham and cheese or egg salad?'

'They both sound good. I forgot to eat breakfast. Coffee?'

'Yes, please.' Alice wandered to the door of the living room. 'That tree is just right there, isn't it?'

'It is. Hope I remember to water it.'

'I'll remind you.' She turned away so quickly it felt like she was avoiding eye contact. 'Or just make a habit of doing it when you do some weekly chore, like putting your bins out.'

Nate had his phone nearby as they sat and ate the sandwiches a short time later, but it remained silent and he barely tasted even the mustard in the ham and cheese. He got Alice to help him choose places to hang some other artwork he had but another hour ticked past with no contact. Alice had, of course, noticed how often he was looking at his phone.

'Text her,' she said, with a smile. 'If she's in Dunedin she won't have any problems with reception and hey…this is about *your* baby. She must know that you'll be hanging out to hear the results.'

Nate picked up his phone. He sent a message.

An hour later, he still hadn't had a response and the tension was getting unbearable.

'Don't feel you need to hang around,' he said apologetically. 'You've probably got a lot you want to get done on your day off and I'm not exactly great company.'

'I'm not going anywhere,' Alice said quietly. Again, it felt like she was avoiding direct eye contact, looking around the room as if hunting for a distraction. Her gaze landed on her shoulder bag. 'Hey… I've got something for you. I totally forgot.'

'You shouldn't be buying anything for me,' Nate told her. 'And I need to know what you spent on all those plants this morning so I can pay you back.'

'Didn't buy these.' Alice had fished something

yellow out of her bag. 'I made them the other night when I was watching a movie.' She bit her lip as she opened her hand. 'Don't laugh at my knitting. It's just a pair of bootees.'

Nate blinked. For some reason, the fact that Alice had created a pair of baby shoes for *his* baby brought a huge lump to his throat. He opened his mouth to say something but a sound interrupted him. They both turned to look down the hallway at the front door. Then they looked at each other.

'It couldn't be,' Alice whispered. '*Could* it?'

Nate didn't say anything. If, for some reason, someone wanted to deliver news in person, it could only be bad.

He went to open the door, his heart sinking. It landed with a thump when he saw who it was.

'Hi, Nate.' His visitor knew she had given him more than merely a surprise. 'Can I come in?'

'*Simone*…' His voice cracked. 'Oh, my God… is something wrong?'

Alice had heard Nate's horrified greeting and she was frozen to the spot, the bootees still in her hand as Simone came into the kitchen, her long, auburn hair flowing loose over her shoulders and a huge smile on her face.

'Donna,' she exclaimed. 'I'm so happy to finally meet you properly.'

Alice opened her mouth to correct her but she could see Nate over Simone's shoulder and there was no mistaking the panic in his eyes as he pushed his fingers through his hair.

This was stunning. For some inexplicable reason, Simone thought she was Donna. What would happen if the truth came out now? When Nate was alone in his house with a woman who wasn't his wife? Just a 'friend'? What assumptions might Simone actually make about why his wife had left? And about how fit he was to be a father, single or otherwise? What if it turned out she hadn't helped Nate at all? That she had, in fact, been responsible for making his worst fears come true?

'It's—ah—good to meet you, Simone,' she managed before she was folded into a hug. She saw Nate mouth something that looked like 'thank you' before he was hidden from view.

She was still frozen. What on earth had she just done? She could feel the roundness of Simone's belly through the soft corduroy dungarees she was wearing.

'I'm so sorry not to have given you any warning,' Simone said. 'But this was such a spur-of-the-moment thing. I was about to ring you, Nate, but Olly had made a video of the whole scan because I felt bad that I had shared it with him instead of you but we knew it would be too big a file to try and send. And Olly had this *brilliant* idea as we started driving south—' Her words were tumbling out with excitement. 'We passed the turn-off to the airport and he said why didn't I just jump on a flight and come and surprise you and when we found there was a seat available and we could make it work, it felt like fate… I can't stay long—only an hour or so. The only flight I could get back was later this afternoon and Olly's waiting at the airport in Dunedin to drive me home.' Simone paused to snatch a breath.

Alice was watching Nate. It looked like he was holding his breath.

'Nothing's wrong,' Simone said happily. 'She's perfect. Guys…' She looked from Nate to Alice and back again. 'Your little girl is absolutely perfect.'

Alice felt tears welling up in her eyes as she saw first a wash of relief and then the glow of joy on Nate's face.

'Aww…' Simone gave her another hug. When she straightened, she looked down at Alice's hands. 'Did *you* knit those adorable bootees?'

Alice nodded. She swiped at a tear before it could escape.

'I used to love knitting,' Simone said. 'Just listening to the click of my needles and dreaming about meeting my baby. I don't get much time for it these days, though.' She took a deep breath, stepping further back. 'I don't imagine you get much time, either, what with having to travel so much for your photo shoots.'

Alice swallowed. Hard. She turned her head to find that Nate was walking towards them. What should she do? How could anyone believe she could be making a career out of looking beautiful enough to model clothes? Nate was holding her gaze. She could almost feel the message he was trying to send.

*Please...don't say anything. Can we pretend? It's only for an hour...*

He stopped right beside her. Close enough for his arm to be pressing against hers. When he took the bootees from her hand, Alice could feel the touch of his skin against hers—an electrical current that was enough to shock her back into life.

She could do this. She had to—for Nate's sake.

'I'm sorry you've found us in such a mess,' she said. 'We've been busy sorting out the last of the house.' She pushed a stray strand of wavy hair back from her face.

'Don't apologise.' Simone flapped a hand. 'It's lovely to see you in real life. Not that I haven't loved the photographs and those glamourous magazine shots. And that wedding picture you sent me a while back. Oh...how romantic was that?'

'You didn't tell me you sent Simone a wedding

photo.' Nate looked as if he might be gritting his teeth for a moment. 'That's almost ancient history.'

'I loved it,' Simone said. 'So romantic, that silhouette of you guys holding hands and watching the sun set.'

A back view photo? The glamour that could be created by makeup and hair artists for magazine shoots? Being in the house with the husband that Simone had already met? It could explain why the assumption that she was, indeed, Donna, had been made, especially when Simone had something more important on her mind.

'Come and see the scan.' Simone pulled a tablet out of her woven straw tote bag. 'Let's not waste any more of the precious minutes we've got. You sit here, Donna—' she pulled out a chair at the dining table '—and you sit here, Nate.' She dragged another chair so that they were side by side. She propped the tablet up on one of the silver candlesticks and tapped the play button.

Alice watched the paler blobs moving on the black background of the screen as the technician angled the transducer to sweep the uterus and find how the baby was lying. Suddenly, and very unexpectedly, a tiny hand was in the centre of the screen for a second. Alice heard the way Nate caught his breath and she could feel the magic of this from his point of view. They both had their hands resting on the table and it took only the smallest shift to let the side of her hand and her little finger to touch his—to let him know that she knew how important this was to him and that it was a privilege to be sharing it with him.

She hadn't expected Nate's hand to slide over hers and his fingers to curl so that they could hold her hand. His eyes were still fixed on the screen.

'That's the skull,' the technician said. 'There's the spine…and…here's the heart.'

They could see the flutter of movement inside the tiny heart and then they could hear the beat—a rapid swish of sound. Nate's fingers tightened on Alice's hand and she squeezed back when she saw the tears in his eyes as he turned his head just far enough to catch her gaze.

*Oh-h...*

It was a feeling like nothing Alice had ever experienced. A connection with another human that was deeper than she'd ever felt. And it felt like the most natural thing in the world to keep holding Nate's hand while the detailed examination of the baby began and views and measurements were taken of the brain and spine, the heart chambers and blood flow and each internal organ and limb were checked.

They sat in stunned silence for a moment as the scan ended.

'Aww…' Simone wiped away a tear. She leaned

to put her own hand on top of where Nate's hand was still gripping Alice's. 'I knew it would be like this for you guys. I'm so glad I came…'

Nate cleared his throat but his voice still sounded hoarse. 'Thank you. I can't tell you how much it means.'

'I can feel it.' Simone pressed her hand to her chest as she got to her feet. 'My taxi's coming back in ten minutes,' she said. 'I can't miss that flight but I really want to see that gorgeous nursery before I go. *Oh…*' She pulled in a gasp of a breath.

'What?' Nate was on his feet now, the physical link between him and Alice finally broken. 'What's wrong?'

'Nothing.' Simone reached out to take his hand. 'Your daughter's woken up, that's all. Here… feel…' She put his hand on her belly and then turned to Alice. 'You, too?' she invited. 'Come and feel her kicking.'

If Alice had thought the connection between herself and Nate had been something extraordinary as they watched his baby on the screen, it paled in comparison to his hand over hers and the baby actually moving beneath her palm and fingers.

The busyness of giving Simone a whirlwind tour of the house, and the nursery in particular, and then going with her to see her into the car meant that there was no time to process what had just happened, and Alice's head was spinning as they stood at the gate to wave her off. Simone was turning to wave at them out of the back window.

'She's still watching us,' Nate said as the car began to move. 'Do you think she really believed that you're Donna?'

'I think so,' Alice said. But then she looked up to catch his gaze. 'But we could make sure.'

She could see the flash of comprehension in his eyes. There was no time to second-guess anything, because they would be out of Simone's view in a matter of moments. Alice found herself stretching up onto her tiptoes. Nate was bending his head to meet her.

The last Simone would see of them was the kiss between an apparently happy couple—the parents-to-be of the baby she was carrying.

It had only needed to last a heartbeat or two but Alice could feel them both falling into this kiss, and it went on for long enough to feel like more than simply a performance for the benefit of someone else.

Unbelievably, for Alice, *this* was going to be the most memorable part of an extraordinary day.

# CHAPTER SEVEN

'Aratika One… Aratika One…you're tasked to a single vehicle crash on Highway 60, south of Tākaka. Male driver, mid-thirties, trapped and unconscious. Police, fire and ambulance on scene…'

Alice and Nate had already begun moving away from the morning briefing as their pagers sounded, before the announcement came over the speaker system as backup communication. Their pilot, Andy, and the crew person Nick were ahead of them.

Alice pulled on her helmet as she crossed the helipad. Nate followed her into the cabin of the helicopter, closed and secured the side door, sat down and put his harness on.

'Crew ready?' Andy's voice was loud in their headphones.

'Crew ready,' Alice confirmed. She had her tablet on her lap. Further information would be arriving to update them as they headed to the scene and she was hoping the patient would have been extricated from the vehicle by the time they arrived. Right now she had the map on her screen that would follow their route across the channel that divided the north and south islands of New Zealand. The accident site was at the tip of the South Island and that made them the closest crew available.

Nate was also adjusting what information he was getting on his tablet but, weirdly, it felt like they both looked up at each other in exactly the same moment. A glance that was held long enough to be significant.

And how could it *not* be significant after what had happened only yesterday?

Oh, they'd made light of that kiss that had been only for show the moment it had ended. Alice had been the first to find some words, probably because she'd been embarrassed. What if Nate thought she was moving in—that she might be interested in taking the idea of pretending that she was his wife even further?

*'Wow...who knew you were such a good actor? That almost felt real...'*

*'I could say the same about you. I completely believed you when we were in the nursery and you told Simone how overwhelming this all was because you'd never thought you'd have the joy of becoming a mother.'*

*'That was probably the most honest thing I said.'*

*'Of course it was.'* Nate's smile had been apologetic. *'I'm sorry I forced you to be part of my deception. It was overwhelming, which was probably why I couldn't see a way out of it fast enough.'*

*'It was me who agreed that it wasn't a problem to wait before you let Simone know you were planning on being a solo parent. It's okay, Nate. I wasn't going to drop you in it and...hey...'* Alice had found her brightest smile. *'I'm not complaining. You're a good kisser. But...it's time I went home. See you at work tomorrow?'*

And that was that. They'd both dismissed the kiss, along with the unspoken connection of watching that scan together and feeling the baby move, as no more than doing what needed to be done to buy Nate a little more time to protect his future.

Something that would never have been real. And something that was never going to happen again.

But…oh, my…it was still there in that brush of eye contact, wasn't it? Alice could still feel an echo of that sensation of falling into something… huge… The attraction that had always been there but had never been allowed to see the light of day had well and truly had its cover ripped off.

It was real. Not that it could come to anything. Alice had no desire to be a mother to any child. Or to be in a relationship where the emotional well-being of a child was any of her responsibility. Why would she, when she could still hear her grandmother's disappointed tone?

*This apple didn't fall far from the tree, did it? You're just like your mother...*

How could she have contradicted that? She hadn't even wanted to take responsibility for a doll when it was what every other little girl wanted to do.

And Nate? Well, he had far bigger things in his life to deal with than the fact that he was single. He probably didn't even feel the need for a sex life right now and, judging by the way he was focussed on the screen of his tablet again, he hadn't allowed any hidden depths in that shared glance to distract him in the slightest from the work ahead of them.

She needed to follow his example.

Could Alice tell?

That he'd been thinking about that kiss every time he looked at her? That he'd been thinking about it even more, last night, when she wasn't even there?

He had been trying to figure out what had made it so...intense and he'd finally decided that it was because Alice had demonstrated—yet again—that she was in his corner by insisting on staying with him when she knew he was getting anxious about the results of that scan. Knowing that she cared that much about how he was feeling had opened up a space in his heart that he'd thought he'd slammed shut recently—a space that was only available to the people he could really trust.

She'd stepped up even more by letting Simone believe that she was Donna. That his marriage was still intact and his baby was going to have an entire family.

But maybe most significantly, Alice had been there when he'd seen his unborn baby for the first time. They'd been linked by skin-to-skin contact as the enormity of seeing his daughter's face and those tiny fingers and hearing her heart beat had brought tears to his eyes and again when her hand had been beneath his to feel the miracle of the baby moving in Simone's belly.

No wonder the emotional connection had been off the charts well before they'd staged that kiss. Adding an intimate touch of lips on lips into the mix had been like lighting a fuse. A long and very unexpected fuse that was leading to a bomb that represented…

Sex, that's what that bomb was.

The closest physical—and emotional—connection any two humans could have.

He shouldn't even be thinking about it but it was impossible not to. Because that kiss had given him the distinct impression that Alice was also aware of that fuse. Letting it reach the bomb would be a disaster. A dead-end road to ruining what was shaping up to be the best friendship he'd ever discovered. A supportive friendship he was going to need very much in his near future.

Nate had done his best to stamp on the spark that was fizzing along that fuse and put it out. He thought he'd been successful. Until he'd arrived at the base this morning, that is. From the moment he'd seen Alice, even before she smiled at him, he had been tapping into his higher levels of determination in order to stay focussed on what he was here to do.

Being tasked with a mission that could prove challenging was exactly what he needed. With a bit of luck, working together would be enough to put things back the way they had been and deal with that disturbing spark once and for all.

Updates coming in were already making this all about what they were heading for on a remote road in the rugged, bush-covered hills between two national parks. The hatchback car had failed to take a corner on the winding road and had rolled down a steep bank to land in a shallow creek, fortunately right way up.

'He's regained consciousness.' Alice's voice was in his earphones. 'GCS up to fourteen now. He's confused but complaining of severe pain in his neck.'

Nate was reading the same messages. 'He can't move his hands or feet. He's going to need a controlled extrication to protect his spine.'

'A paramedic's managed to climb in through the back hatch. He's got cervical spine immobilisation in place and oxygen on.'

'The fire service is planning to remove the roof to allow for the extrication. Do we have an idea of how long that's going to take?'

'They've only just stabilised the vehicle with chocks and a winch. Be lucky if they've got him out before we get there.'

'At least we've got a place to land.' Andy joined the conversation. 'There's a passing lane that widens the road after that corner and a picnic area that leads down to that creek.'

There was no chance of Nate being distracted by anything that wasn't purely professional by the time they landed a few hundred metres from the accident scene and made their way along the road that was now closed to general traffic in both directions and clogged with emergency service vehicles, including an ambulance and first response unit, fire trucks and several police cars. Personnel who weren't down the bank were standing at the top, watching what was going on.

For the next thirty minutes, that was all Nate and Alice could do as well because there was no room for any extra medics in or around the vehicle. The roof had been cut and folded back and the driver, in a rigid extrication jacket and hard collar, was being strapped to a backboard, with further neck immobilisation from soft blocks, secured by bandaging, on either side of his head. It took six people, mostly fire officers who were the experts in extrication, to lift the backboard and carefully inch the victim clear of the car's interior and the sharp edges of the twisted metal. Still on the backboard, he was lowered into a Stokes rescue basket and secured, padded and covered with blankets for warmth. Lines were attached to winch the basket up the steep bank and, finally, Nate and Alice were able to meet their patient and do their own assessments as they took over his care for transport.

It was Alice who crouched beside the rescue basket.

'Hi… I'm Alice. I'm a paramedic. And that's Nate there, who's a doctor. You're Ben, aren't you?'

'Yeah.'

'How are you feeling?'

'C-cold…'

'Anything hurting?'

'Just my neck. I… I can't feel anything else…' There was a note of terror in Ben's voice. 'I'm never going to be able to walk again, am I?'

Alice took hold of Ben's hand. Could he feel that? Nate knew what it felt like. How reassuring it could be.

'I know how scary this is,' she said. 'You've got an injury to your neck but we can't know how serious it is yet. What we're going to do is take the very best care of you and keep you safe until we get to the specialists.'

Nate moved so that he was right beside Alice. Crouched down close enough to touch Ben's shoulder. Alice was still holding his hand. 'You're breathing on your own,' he said. 'Your heart rate's good and we're happy with your blood pressure. You've had a nasty crash but you're doing really well. Try and focus on that and let us take care of you.'

He glanced sideways to find Alice's gaze on him. There was a softness to her mouth and eyes that suggested she approved of the reassurance he was offering.

Ben tried to nod his head but Nate put his hand on his forehead. 'Try and keep your head completely still,' he said. 'How's that pain in your neck?'

'Bad.'

'On a scale of zero to ten, with zero being no pain and ten being the worst you can imagine, what score would you give it?'

'Nine.'

'Okay. We're going to give you something for that and then we're going to shift you onto our stretcher for the helicopter. We've got a special mattress on it that we can take the air out of and it moulds around your body to keep you still and protect your neck.'

Alice had moved as he was speaking and, when Nate looked up again, she was unzipping the IV pack, ready to hand him everything he needed to establish a line and give Ben some pain relief and fluids.

'Thanks, Alice.' His smile was as subtle as hers had been only seconds ago but he was grateful for more than her anticipating what was needed next. This was exactly how it needed to be during working hours in a valued partnership where skills and knowledge were shared to the benefit of all.

No undercurrents.

No fizzing fuses.

Professional.

By the time they'd got back to base after delivering Ben to the nearest major trauma centre that could take care of an acute spinal injury and provide the intensive care and possibly surgery that Ben would require, it was halfway through their morning.

'It's Saturday,' Andy said happily as he began the helicopter's shutdown. 'Do you think Shirley's made cheese scones?'

'What's her story?' Nate asked as he walked into the hangar with Alice. 'How did she get so involved with the rescue base? I've never asked her.'

'She's a legend,' Alice told him. 'As much a part of the place as any crew members. You should ask her one day. She loves telling the story of her son who went tramping about twenty years ago and fell down a cliff. He would have died if he hadn't been winched out in the nick of time. She brought a cake in to thank the crew and it just grew from there. Cakes, scones, cookies. Getting involved with any fundraising that was going on.'

'She seems to practically live here,' Nate said. 'Not that I'm complaining. Closest thing I've had to a mum around for a very long time.'

'It's the people connection that she needed, too, I think. Her son moved away. To the States. But it was after her husband died that Shirley started coming in a lot more. We're her family. She must be well into her seventies now but, man, she can cope with anything—even a Sunday roast dinner for about fifteen people.' She grinned at Nate. 'I want to be Shirley when I grow up.'

The sound of Nate's laughter as he reached to pull the door open made Alice's heart thump as it made up for a missed beat. Or was it that she'd caught his gaze and the eye contact felt like a physical touch. She had to look away. Otherwise she was going to start thinking about that kiss. Again.

What made them both look away was the sound of their pagers going off. Nate was holding the door open with his shoulder as they read the message but then he stepped away and let it close again. They shared another glance that was an acknowledgement they weren't going to get a coffee and one of Shirley's cheese scones anytime soon, and they both turned to walk back to the helicopter.

'No rest for the wicked today,' Alice said brightly. 'We love Saturdays when everyone's out doing their sports and recreation.'

They barely got time for a late lunch. It was one job after another. A bad fall on the cross-country course at an equestrian event left a teenage girl with a head injury and rib fractures. A man suffered a heart attack climbing a steep hill track and was more than an hour's drive away from a hospital so needed urgent transport. A woman with a low-lying placenta had gone into early labour and was bleeding heavily and, just when their shift was due to finish, they were tasked to a car crash but stood down when an ambulance crew arrived on scene and found there were no serious injuries.

It was even later by the time they'd cleaned up and restocked but people were still busy getting sick and injured. As Alice was peeling off her overalls and boots in the locker room and putting her street shoes on, she heard the clatter of the night shift crew heading out of the hangar. The whine of a helicopter's engine warming up outside distracted her slightly as she pulled the locker room door open and maybe that explained why she walked straight into Nate, who was coming on his way in.

'Oh…' The warmth of him hit her like a solid wave, followed instantly by a memory of how it felt to be even closer to this man. 'Sorry,' she added, hastily. 'I wasn't thinking.'

Alice had taken a step back. Nate was still in the doorway. They'd both stopped moving. Alice could hear the rotors gathering speed now and feel the steady thump of displaced air reverberating through the huge hangar. It felt like a heartbeat.

Or perhaps she was feeling her own heartbeat. Because she'd lifted her gaze to Nate's. After a long moment, his gaze dropped to her lips. And then it lifted again and Alice knew.

He was thinking about the kiss.

The noise outside was loud enough to drown the gasp of Alice's indrawn breath. Maybe she imagined the low growl that came from Nate as he stepped closer and pushed the locker door closed behind him without breaking that eye contact. Alice lifted her face, her lips parting and Nate bent his head and still their gazes were locked. Until they were too close to be able to see each other but it didn't matter because that wasn't what either of them wanted.

They wanted to *feel* the touch of each other's lips. To go back to the taste of something extraordinary that they'd been left with yesterday. To find out if there really was something that could justify a magnetic pull that was this powerful.

There was nothing staged about this kiss. Alice was letting herself fall, further and further into this pool of sensation. The softness of Nate's lips, the glide of his tongue. She could feel his hands holding her face and then moving over her body but it still felt utterly safe—as if he was catching her as she fell.

The helicopter was long gone when they both pulled back to try and catch a breath.

Alice definitely heard a groan from Nate this

time. His voice was low. Roughened by what sounded like desire.

'Is it my turn to apologise?'

'No...'

Dear Lord...how had they managed to pretend there was nothing significant about that kiss yesterday? The tension in the air between them at the moment was so thick it was hard to breathe.

'Good,' Nate growled. 'Because I want to kiss you again.'

Alice couldn't say anything. She couldn't find the words that would encompass how much she wanted him to.

'But I don't want to ruin our friendship,' Nate said. 'You've been amazing, Alice, and...an absolute rock and I can't tell you how much I appreciate everything you've—'

'Nate?' Alice interrupted.

He blinked. 'What?'

Alice reached up and put her hands around his neck. 'Just shut up,' she told him. 'And kiss me again.'

There was pretty much zero danger of being disturbed. Administration staff and the other day crew members had left some time ago. The night crew of a paramedic, crewman and pilot were who knew where, flying towards an emergency that had the extra challenge of being a scene cloaked in darkness.

The operations manager on shift was nowhere near the hangar or locker rooms and they would be focussed on monitoring updates from the current mission, tracking where the helicopter was and fielding any other incoming calls.

Not that Nate was actually thinking that straight.

He wasn't thinking of anything other than *this…*

This astonishing response from this woman in his arms. The scent and taste of her. The taut muscles of her back as she pressed into him. The incredible softness of her breasts against his body. The tiny sounds she was making.

The *heat…*

Okay…a tiny alarm bell was sounding. They did need more privacy. Preferably their own scene that was cloaked in darkness. Somehow it didn't surprise him at all that Alice picked up on the thought the moment it occurred to him. Or had he picked up on hers? They broke the kiss to stare at each other. It was a moment that either of them could have used to slow things down. Back off completely, even.

But that eye contact only seemed to be ramping up the heat. Nate could almost imagine a flicker of flames like an aura around their bodies.

'An on-call room?' Alice suggested in a whisper. 'Upstairs?'

'Through the staff room?' Nate shook his head, albeit reluctantly.

The night-shift operations manager would be upstairs somewhere. They might both be off-duty and single, consenting adults but Nate didn't want this to become an item of gossip. Alice had made the assumption that he'd been having an affair when he'd told her that he was a father to a baby that wasn't Donna's. If anyone saw them together they might make even wilder assumptions—like that Alice had been a part of why his marriage had failed? Keeping this private was a way he could protect Alice and, no matter how powerful this physical attraction might be, he had every intention of protecting Alice.

Alice was shaking *her* head now, but it wasn't for a negative reason.

'The fire escape.' Her gaze went to the spiral staircase in the corner of the hangar, which provided access to the platform built into the wall that was used for winch training purposes. Nate had never done any winch training, so he'd never had any reason to notice the door at the top that must lead into a corridor that led to the staffroom and offices. A space that divided the bedrooms on either side that were provided for any base crews on call overnight.

An almost secret passage.

As exciting as the thought of taking this connection with Alice to the next level. Did she want that as much as he did? But was it still risking too much to give in to this overpowering pull right now?

'Come home with me,' he said softly.

'You want to wait *that* long?'

Nate could feel his smile beginning to curl as any doubts evaporated. Yeah…she *did* want this just as much as he did. He didn't have to say anything aloud. She took one look at that smile and grabbed his hand. Seconds later they were at the top of the staircase, opening the first door they came to and slipping inside without bothering to even try and find a light switch.

How perfect was this?

Sex, spiced with a level of physical attraction like none Alice had ever experienced. A totally gorgeous man who clearly knew what he was doing. The way he could kiss—as if he was savouring the most delicious treat imaginable and he wanted to make it last as long as possible.

The way he was touching her! Sliding his hands inside her clothing, removing that clothing with far more skill than she was demonstrating as she fumbled with the stud on his jeans and then…oh, *my*…his fingers on her bare skin—gently tracing the shape of her body as if he needed to be sure that his touch was welcome and then, when Alice had been ready to beg for more, holding her with a strength that made it impossible not to surrender completely and simply melt into his arms.

It was a rollercoaster of sensation like nothing she'd ever known. Nate had a talent for finding a way of eliciting a stifled groan of delight and then teasing her, making her wait a beat and then, somehow, taking it to a whole new level. The release, when it came, was another revelation of just how good sex could be.

It wasn't until she was trying to catch her breath, some time later, that Alice realised what might be adding so much to this pleasure.

There was no hidden agenda. Neither of them was taking tentative steps towards a possible relationship. They liked each other. They fancied each other and…they trusted each other enough to make this safe.

Safe and so astonishingly *good*…

Alice could feel the rapid pulse of Nate's heartbeat finally beginning to slow as she lay pressed against his body in this narrow, single bed. Had he found it as good as she had? Would he want to do it again? As much as she did?

When she looked up, he had that smile on his face again. That drop-dead sexy smirk that he'd had in that moment before they'd made a dash for the fire-escape staircase.

'My place next time?' he murmured. 'I've got a much nicer bed.'

# CHAPTER EIGHT

IT *WAS* HIS place the next time.

Hers, the time after that.

It should have been enough to have taken the edge off any curiosity about each other and blunted what they had both acknowledged was a friendship with a surprisingly strong streak of lust involved but, in fact, it seemed to be having the opposite effect. The more they discovered, the better they got to know each other, the more irresistible the sex became.

One week slipped into another with no signs of the attraction being sated. It felt more like a growing addiction.

It could never last, of course. They both knew that. There was a ticking clock in the background. Nate was going to become a single father and his life would never be this relaxed out of work hours. He'd probably be too tired for any desire for sex to be registered, let alone acted upon and perhaps that became an unspoken excuse to be together—to make the most of it before it evaporated. This bubble of time had an expiry date.

It wasn't only the pleasure of the sex that was filling the bubble. What came alongside the physical intimacy—the deepening of their friendship and the trust between them—was something that felt like it could last a lifetime.

Something precious.

As that level of trust grew, the words they could share were sometimes an echo of the closeness they had discovered with physical touch. Part of the safety net of knowing they weren't in a 'real' relationship meant that Nate could talk to her about the crushing disintegration of his marriage and she loved that she could, completely sincerely, offer reassurance that he couldn't blame himself.

Like tonight, when they were sitting in the dark, watching the lights of the city from the windows in Nate's house, sharing a bottle of wine and having an animated conversation about the interesting cases they'd been involved with that day.

Nate stopped with a shake of his head. 'No wonder Donna got so sick of my talking shop. I'm married to my job as much as I was ever married to her.'

'You're a passionate person—that's why you're so good at what you do. I'd be willing to bet that was what attracted her to you in the first place. You're determined to be the best you can be and you're already good enough to be better than anyone else I've ever worked with and that's not just because you're so smart. It's because you're...' Alice smiled at him. 'You're a nice guy, Nate. You're compassionate. You have a lot of love to give and—' her smile widened '—you're going to be an amazing dad.'

Nate made a face. 'I had every intention of being an amazing husband, too. Where did I go wrong? Was it because I wasn't prepared to let go of the dream of having a family?'

Alice stared out at the lights for a long moment. She could see an emergency vehicle, probably a police car, racing along the main road leading away from the city.

'If you're with someone who doesn't want the same things from life as you do, it's inevitable that you'll drift apart. It's nobody's fault. And if they're really big things like whether or not you want kids, it's never going to work. Nobody can live their best life if they're unhappy.'

'But why did she agree to the surrogacy? I really thought that was going to give us a second chance.'

'I'm sure she did, too. Maybe she felt guilty about the affair and that it was *her* fault your marriage was in trouble and this was her way of trying to fix it. She cared enough about you to try but, as you said, when it became a reality, that was when she had to admit the truth—that it wasn't what she wanted.'

'It was a bit late by then, though, wasn't it?'

Alice took in a deep breath. 'You're both getting a second chance to be the people you want to be,' she pointed out quietly. 'She's chasing the career she wants so much. And you're going to be a dad.'

'I am, aren't I?'

Nate's smile began slowly but Alice could see he was now looking forwards, not backwards. She got the impression that he was feeling a lot happier than he had moments ago.

She brushed off a feeling of pride that she'd had something to do with making him feel good. It was just what friends did, wasn't it?

Nate shared the regular updates Simone sent him, like a text message with a laughing face emoji that said his daughter was kicking her so hard now she was beginning to wonder if she was destined to join the New Zealand Black Ferns who were the country's international women's rugby team.

It was definitely a step too far for Alice to send messages to Simone herself, pretending that they were coming from Donna but she helped write messages that they knew would be taken as coming from both parents-to-be.

Like the one that was about the child-sized table and chairs they'd found in a junk shop and taken home to paint in bright, primary colours. The table was blue and the little wooden chairs were red and yellow and green. Alice had taken a picture of Nate with smears of paint on his hands and a proud smile on his face. Alice had found an equally bright, plastic tea set online and they'd set them out on the little blue table when the paint was dry. A small teapot, milk jug, and cups and saucers, along with a few cupcakes that were pink and white and as sparkly as any princess could desire.

*Just practising*, Nate had captioned the photos. *Next time we might even bake the cupcakes ourselves.*

Simone sent a picture of her bump the following week and, when she was transitioning into her third trimester not long after that, she emailed all the blood test and other results from her midwifery check.

*It's all going so well*, she wrote. *And I know you'll both be as happy as we are. Carrying your baby feels like the best decision I ever made.*

Alice was happier than she'd ever been but it wasn't only because of how smoothly the surrogate pregnancy was going. Or that she was enjoying the best sex life she'd ever discovered and building a lifelong friendship.

Life in general just seemed to be particularly enjoyable at the moment. Work was more satisfying than ever, especially on the days she was crewed with Nate. They'd always had the connection that allowed them to work seamlessly together, not only making the most of each other's skills and knowledge but allowing them to improve as well.

Like the time he coached her through a particularly difficult intubation on a patient with major facial trauma when she thought a surgical airway might be the only option.

*Measure the distance between incisors. Three fingers is enough room for the laryngoscope.*

*I'll keep the field as clear as I can with suction for you. Use the bougie even if you can only see the epiglottis. Feel for the clicks of the tracheal rings.*

The satisfaction of securing that airway had been something that Alice would use as encouragement to tackle a difficult challenge for the rest of her career.

The pride from Nate's nod and the quiet praise of 'good job' had taken a small moment in her life and transformed it into something she would remember for the rest of her life.

She might only have an evening with Nate

once or twice a week but it was enough. Keeping their alliance discreet added an extra level to the pleasure of working together and the infrequency of their private time together increased the level of anticipation for it to be a noticeable factor in how alive she was feeling these days.

Life had never been quite this good before.

Nate looked happier than he had in a long time, too, and Alice wasn't the only person to notice, but then Shirley had a sharp eye when it came to what was going on with the people she loved to care about on the Aratika Rescue Base.

'It's good to see you with a bit more spring in your step, lad,' she told him, putting a plate with one of everyone's favourite breakfast bacon rolls on it. She leaned down and spoke more quietly but Alice was sitting close enough to overhear what she said. 'You've had a tough time of it, lately, haven't you?' She patted his arm. 'You deserve better and that's all I have to say about it.'

Alice and Nate shared a glance. It was highly unlikely that Shirley wouldn't have more to say about it in the not-too-distant future but nobody minded her treading on personal ground. She was a real mother-figure on the base and well-loved.

They didn't get to finish their breakfast that morning, however. The strident sound of pagers going off had the crew moving fast towards the operations room where Don held up his hand to signal that he wasn't finished with the phone call he was taking. He was watching information being added to the computer screen in front of him at the same time. Alice and Nate were scrolling their tablets, getting the same updates. Andy was already checking weather reports on his device.

'Where's Nick?' Alice asked.

'He's called in sick. Sounds like food poisoning and there's no replacement available as yet.'

'Right…' Don's tone was crisp. 'As you can see, we've got a twenty-four-year-old woman who's thirty-six weeks pregnant. Has a low-lying posterior placenta and was down for an elective C-section at thirty-eight weeks. She's bleeding.' Don paused for a beat. 'She's on the Cape Palliser Coast. In Ngawi.'

Alice's head jerked up. 'Wow…that's about as isolated as you can get around here.'

Ngawi was a tiny fishing village on the southeastern base of the North Island, sandwiched between rugged hills and the sea. It had a small population of permanent residents rather than holidaymakers and it was famous for the tractors lined up on the shingle beach to haul fishing boats ashore.

Don nodded. 'Nearest GP or first responders are more than an hour away. You'll get to them in half the time they would need to take off in a car to meet an ambulance en route.'

'She's getting intermittent contractions,' Nate noted. 'But there's no indication of any trauma?'

'She's got UTI symptoms.' Alice was scrolling her tablet again. 'That can precipitate labour.'

Don was looking at Andy now. 'Cloud ceiling's currently just over eight hundred feet at Ngawi, with wind gusts up to thirty-five knots. Marginal VFR given the hilly terrain.'

Both Alice and Nate looked up this time. They knew that if they couldn't fly with the visual flight rules they needed for a safe distance from the ground, Andy could refuse to accept the mission.

'I wouldn't want the ceiling to get any lower,' he said. 'But we'll give it a go. From what I can see here, there looks like a good landing area beside the community hall or in the camping grounds over the road. Is there a local cop who can make sure it's currently clear and keep bystanders away?'

'No local police. They're as far away as the nearest medical help in Martinborough. I'll get Comms onto it. They can contact the manager of the camping grounds or maybe the person who's in charge of the rural fire station.'

The briefing had taken less than two minutes and the process of getting from the operations room to the helipad wasn't going to take much longer than that, even when they were collecting their gear and the extra supplies they might need. Like blood products.

Especially blood products.

'If she is in labour she's also at high risk of a postpartum haemorrhage.' The glance Nate gave Alice had an edge she'd never seen before but she recognised it instantly.

This felt personal to him. Running into trouble in late pregnancy, somewhere where advanced medical care was a long way away, could be catastrophic.

Simone lived in an isolated area.

'Crew ready?' Andy had the helicopter ready for lift-off by the time Nate and Alice were clipping into their harnesses.

'Ready.'

'We recommend that you keep those safety belts fastened at all times while seated, in case of unexpected turbulence.'

Alice's huff of laughter was audible. She knew that Andy loved a bit of rough weather and those wind gusts over hills and around coastal cliffs were more than likely to deliver some buffeting and downdrafts. Was that why Nate wasn't sharing the amusement of Andy's tongue-in-cheek instruction? Or was he worried that they were heading to a potentially serious case minus a crew member—to a case that might be very close to his own heart?

Andy wasn't joking now. He was on a different channel. 'Aratika One to Wellington Tower. We're ready for departure to Ngawi. Requesting clearance.'

'Cleared for take-off, Aratika One. Track east of harbour, not above fifteen hundred feet.'

Alice caught Nate's glance and offered a reassuring smile.

*I've got your back*, she tried to convey. *We've got this.*

It was one of the bumpiest rides Nate had experienced in his time working as a HEMS doctor but that kind of suited his mood.

This could be a high-stakes scenario for both a mother and a baby and, okay, he was possibly more invested on a personal level than he should be but that was inevitable, wasn't it? Just like it would be for any medic going to a situation that had important links to their private lives, especially when it involved the most vulnerable patients. He might have to live with this for the rest of his life, dealing with babies coming into the emergency department and then toddlers and children. Teenagers, even. He suspected this was part and parcel of becoming a parent, and now was as good a time as any to start learning how to deal with it and push any emotional reaction into a space that would have no effect on his professional decisions or skills.

It turned out that it wasn't an issue at all as soon as he walked into the room where Nicole, the young mother, was sitting on the floor of her living area—a large bloodstain visible on the dress she was wearing. Her eyes were closed and her skin very pale.

Nate crouched beside her and took hold of her wrist to take her pulse. 'Hi, Nicole. My name's Nate,' he told her. 'I'm a doctor. I've got Alice with me and we're both here to take care of you and get you to hospital, okay?'

Nicole made a strangled sound, gave up trying to speak and nodded instead. Her face was scrunched into lines of pain.

'Are you having a contraction at the moment?'

Another nod.

Alice was reaching for Nicole's other hand. 'Squeeze my hand,' she said. 'Try and breathe through it.'

Nicole's husband, Gareth, had met them at the door moments ago and relayed the information that the contractions seemed to be getting stronger and more frequent. Nate glanced at his watch so they would know how close together the contractions were. A vaginal examination was contraindicated with any antepartum bleeding because touching the cervix could break blood vessels and turn a small bleed into something far more dangerous.

'Can we get a BP and O2 sats, please, Alice? And some nasal prongs for oxygen. Throw me the IV roll, too, would you?'

'No worries.'

Nicole was opening her eyes as the contraction faded and Alice was already turning to open pouches on the defibrillator case. She pulled out the blood pressure cuff to wrap around Nicole's arm. As the cuff inflated, she unfurled the tubing of nasal prongs and fitted them into nostrils and around ears.

'You're doing really well,' she said, with a smile.

Nate was keeping his voice deliberately calm but his mind was racing. He needed to establish a wide-bore intravenous access. Preferably two. He wanted fluids running and some tranexamic acid administered.

'I'm going to pop a needle into your arm, Nicole,' he told their patient. 'We're going to need to give you some fluids and medication. Is that okay?'

'Y-yes...'

'Have you been feeling unwell in the last few days?'

'Just since I got up. It hurt to pee.'

Nate had swabbed the skin over a large vein in her arm. 'Sharp scratch,' he warned. He slid the tip of needle in and then gently pushed the cannula into place. 'All done.'

Alice was setting up the bag of IV fluids. They had carried in the polystyrene container that kept blood products cool along with all the other gear. Just in case.

'She kept having to go back to the loo every few minutes.' Gareth was hovering near his wife, looking very anxious. 'And that was when she found she was bleeding.'

'BP one-ten over sixty,' Alice relayed. 'Oxygen saturation 97 percent.'

So far so good, Nate thought. He caught Alice's glance. 'Let's get Nicole into a left lateral position until we're ready to load and go.' The less time they spent on scene here, the happier he would be. He reached for the drug kit to extract the medication that could reduce the bleeding. 'An estimate for the blood loss would be helpful.'

He was drawing up the TXA as Alice helped Nicole to lie down and put a cushion beneath her head.

'I'm going to find a fresh pad for you,' she said. 'This one's getting pretty soaked.'

That told Nate that the blood loss could be significant already. Another glance at his watch told him that it had been over two minutes since the last contraction and he blew out a tiny breath that could have been relief. It would be better for everyone if this baby stayed where it was until they were a lot closer to all the equipment and expertise a major obstetrics department could provide.

His relief had been premature.

The slightly surprised sound that came from Alice made his skin prickle. She'd seen something unexpected and was deliberately trying to sound calm, as he had been earlier.

'Um… Nate?'

'Yep?'

He pushed the last drops of the medication out of the syringe into the cannula port and then shifted far enough to see what Alice was looking at.

A dark shape, with whorls of wet hair, that was unmistakably a baby's head crowning.

They weren't going anywhere just yet.

'Nicole?'

'What is it? Is something wrong?'

'Not wrong, but your baby is very close to being born—maybe with the next contraction.'

'*No!*' Nicole sounded horrified. 'That can't happen. I'm supposed to have a Caesarean.' She burst into tears.

Gareth was staring at them, shocked.

'Come and help Nicole,' Alice told him. 'Sit

behind her and she can lean against you and hold your hand.'

Nicole was gasping between her sobs. And then the sound became a cry of pain.

'I have to *push*,' she cried, seconds later.

Nate knelt beside Alice. He cupped his hand over the baby's head, providing a gentle pressure to stop it emerging too rapidly. He felt the cord around the neck but it was loose enough to slip over the head.

'One more push, Nicole,' he said. He guided the head down and then up, to deliver the shoulders and the baby came out with a rush of blood that made Nate's heart sink. Alice had a clean towel in her hands and she met his gaze for a heartbeat as he put the baby onto it. This was the worst-case scenario. A postpartum haemorrhage to deal with so far away from hospital and...a very flat-looking baby.

Alice put the baby boy onto Nicole's chest but she was using the towel to rub the skin on his back and chest briskly, trying to stimulate the newborn.

'Why isn't he crying?' Nicole lifted her head and then dropped it back against her husband. 'Oh... *God*...something's wrong, isn't it?'

'Why is he so *blue*?' Gareth sounded just as horrified.

'It can take a minute or two.' It was only because Nate knew Alice so well that he could hear the note of fear in her voice. He saw her flick the baby's feet and then start rubbing again. 'It's a big transition, coming into the world, especially if it happens a bit fast. His heart rate is good, his breathing just needs to catch up.'

He wasn't only blue. From the corner of his eye, Nate could see Alice shifting the position of the head to make sure the airway was open and he could tell that the baby was completely limp, his eyes shut. He had to leave the initial resuscitative attempt to Alice, however. Nicole's welfare was his priority and he needed to deal with the heavy, ongoing bleeding. There were drugs, including oxytocin and more TXA that needed to be administered, IV fluids and blood products to be infused. Nate wanted an update of all vital signs and the uterus would need to be massaged—compressed, even, if the bleeding continued to be severe and Nicole's condition was deteriorating. It might well be a tense trip back to the city. As soon as he had a few free seconds he would radio Andy and get him to have the chopper ready for take-off and to heat the cabin as much as possible. It couldn't have been a worse call-out to be short of an extra pair of hands to deal with this.

They were not out of the woods yet, that was for sure.

* * *

Alice had never been this afraid.

Her efforts to stimulate this baby seemed to be failing.

It was the bluest, floppiest baby she had ever held in her hands and…it was terrifying.

How devastating would it be to lose this infant? She could see the shock and fear in the faces of both these young parents, and she hoped she wasn't showing how concerned she was herself. And what about Nate? He was already invested in this case on a personal level. She *had* to succeed. She was trying to think ahead to what she needed to do as the next priorities. She needed to know the heart rate, and the oxygen level. Provide ventilation. Clamp and cut the cord? Start CPR?

She rubbed harder with the towel.

'Come on, sweetheart,' she said aloud. 'Take a nice, big breath for me…'

A sideways glance showed her that Nate was flat out drawing up drugs, adjusting the IV. As much as she desperately wanted him to come and help her, she knew she was on her own for the moment. The mother's life took priority. As if he'd felt her glance, Nate looked up. The eye contact was so brief it barely happened but it was enough.

Alice wasn't really on her own, was she?

They were doing this together. And they were

a team that had proved their strength time and time again.

And, just as she had that comforting thought, she felt the baby move beneath her hands. Saw the tiny mouth open and heard the first air being dragged into the baby's lungs.

'That's the way.' Her whisper was fervent. 'Come on, baby.'

The first warbling sound from the infant made Nate's gaze swerve up from where he was injecting medication into the IV line. It shifted from the baby's still-blue face to Nicole, who had buried her face against Gareth's shoulder as they shared their relief at hearing their baby begin to cry and then, finally, it caught Alice's gaze and the message she received was so clear, it might as well have been said aloud.

*Good job... I knew you could do it...*

Another breath and a stronger cry and the dreadful shade of the baby's skin began to change. Pink was fighting the blue and, best of all, the eyes were open. The baby was looking right at Alice. She wanted to put the infant skin-to-skin with his mother as soon as possible, to help keep him warm and to reassure Nicole because her distress could only make her own condition worse but, instead, she held the baby close to her own chest. She had to make sure it was safe to put the baby down and she needed to know that the heart rate was at least a hundred beats per minute.

She cuddled the baby, still wrapped in the towel, her fingers around a tiny arm to feel for the brachial pulse. The baby stopped crying and hiccupped instead, his gaze fixed on Alice's, his face a much healthier colour now.

'You're fine, aren't you, sweetheart?' she said. 'You were just a bit slow to get used to the world.'

The relief was almost overwhelming. She could tuck the baby against his mother's chest, clamp and cut the cord and cover them both to keep warm. Then she would be able to help Nate with whatever he was doing to control any ongoing bleeding. But, for a moment, Alice couldn't move. She couldn't let go of this baby just yet. She was so aware of his warmth and weight in her arms and the rapid beat of his heart against her fingertips. But, more than that, she was totally captured by the way he was looking at her with eyes that were too dark to be able to discern what their colour would be. He could *see* her and Alice was suddenly aware of a connection that was doing strange things to her. Creating a sensation that she'd never felt before.

A yearning that was so deep, it was profound. It felt like *this* was what life was all about.

For the first time in her life, Alice was feeling the desire to have her own baby and it was so unexpected and so strong, it caught her unawares and that made it terrifying.

She had to move and she did so with the confidence that she knew she had. That wash of emotion had been so fleeting nobody could have noticed she was doing anything more than assessing this baby.

'Heart rate's over a hundred,' she reported. 'Sat's are 82 percent and I'd put the five-minute Apgar at eight.'

'Fantastic.' Nate was smiling at Nicole as she gathered her baby into her arms but Alice could see the shadow in his eyes that reminded her of the personal undercurrents here.

She could also still feel the echo of that astonishing wave of her own emotion when she'd been holding this baby.

It felt like something was changing.

Something that Alice didn't *want* to change, because it felt as if the whole foundation of her life was in danger of crumbling.

# CHAPTER NINE

IT STAYED WITH Nate for the rest of what felt like a very long day.

A clear image in his head that came with a wave of something emotional enough for him to know he'd never forget it.

The surprising thing was that it had come from a totally unexpected direction.

It hadn't been the satisfaction, or maybe relief, that he and Alice had managed an out-of-hospital obstetric emergency well enough to have possibly saved two lives today. Nate had rung the hospital for an update just before they left the base to learn that both Nicole and baby Edward were now tucked up in a maternity ward, basking in the afterglow of creating a brand new family.

They'd been on scene longer than anticipated to get Nicole stable enough to transport and then they'd hung around until they got another call so that they could get an update on their patients. Nicole had needed to go to Theatre for the removal of the placenta and definitive control of her bleeding, and the baby boy, Edward, had been taken to NICU for a brief period of observation.

The generous platefuls of Shirley's much-loved Sunday roast that she had kept warm in the oven so that Nate and Alice could have a late lunch when they finally got back to base had been very much appreciated. The delicious roast beef with all the trimmings, including Yorkshire puddings and made-from-scratch gravy, was definitely memorable but that wasn't what he was still thinking about.

No…

The image that had been slotted into a memory bank that was kept for really significant things was that of Alice holding baby Edward. That moment after the baby's first cry, when the horrible fear that they might not win the battle to resuscitate the shocked newborn began to fade rapidly, and Alice was holding the baby in her arms to check his pulse and calculate that first Apgar score.

The way she was cradling the baby in her arms. The way she was looking at that tiny, crumpled face. As if it was her own baby.

As if it was the one thing she'd been waiting for to make her life complete.

She might not know it herself, Nate had thought in that instant, but if she really thought a family was the last thing she wanted, she couldn't be more wrong.

Maybe that was why, when he took her home that evening, the first thing he did after pushing the front door closed behind them, was to take Alice in his arms and simply hold her close. It was Alice who broke what had become an overly long silence.

'I don't think I've ever been quite that scared on a job,' she confessed. 'There was a moment when I thought we might lose them both.'

'You and me both,' Nate murmured. 'But we didn't. How good is that?'

Alice pulled back far enough to see his face. 'I know it was hard on you,' she said quietly. 'I wasn't going to say anything in front of anyone but...you must have been thinking about Simone living so far from a hospital. And you'd know how terrified Nicole and Gareth must have been, knowing that their baby was in danger.'

'It did feel different,' Nate admitted. 'But I knew it was something I had to learn to deal with. I think it's there for every parent—that fear that something might happen that they can't protect their children from.'

Alice's gaze slid away from his. She was nodding but he could sense that she wasn't comfortable talking, or perhaps even thinking, about it. Because she'd been denied the ability to trust that she'd been wrapped in that kind of protection when she'd been a child? His breath caught in his chest again. To be allowed to think that it was her fault her mother was less than happy was worse than her not being loved as much as she'd deserved.

What he wanted more than anything for Alice was that she could find someone to offer that kind of protection to her now. He wished he could offer it himself but they didn't have that kind of relationship, did they? That kind of commitment to protection and safety were the bonds of family and Nate had not forgotten what Alice had said to him in the first truly personal conversation they'd ever had—that she'd grown up thinking that life would be so much better if you didn't have a family.

It was heartbreaking that she'd never been offered the kind of unconditional love that family could provide. How could she know that the risks that came from both giving and receiving that kind of love were so absolutely worth it?

He needed to steer the conversation back to the question Alice had asked.

'Any background thoughts of Simone or the baby were gone the moment we arrived,' he added. 'There's nothing like a medical emergency to push any personal considerations away, is there?'

He saw the tiniest flicker of something in Alice's eyes which suggested that she was remembering the very personal moment for herself but it was gone almost before he saw it properly. In its wake, he thought he could see a beat of confusion. Or sadness, even?

Whatever it was, it made him want to wrap Alice in something that was going to make her feel good again. He might not be able to tell her that she had as much of his protection—and his trust—that he could give her as a friend, but maybe his kiss could convey a hint of it. It was a soft kiss. Tender.

'It was a privilege to work with you today, Alice Barlow.' He pushed a stray wave of hair back from her face. 'You really are something special.'

He didn't give her time to respond, because he knew she would deny it. Instead, he kissed her again. With just as much feeling but a little more heat.

'You hungry?' he asked when he broke the contact.

'After one of Shirley's Sunday dinners?' Alice was smiling. 'Not likely. You?'

'Oh… I'm *so* hungry,' Nate said softly.

That was her line, they both knew that but he'd been unable to resist borrowing it. Alice's smile was fading. Judging by the way the pupils in her eyes dilated and her lips parted, she had a very good idea what he was about to add to that line.

'But not for food…'

Oh, my…

Alice had lost count of how many times she and Nate had been to bed together over the last weeks. She'd given up trying to define what it was that made it so good, and simply put it down to their chemistry being particularly well-matched and the level of attraction being off the charts—along with that extra dollop of knowing that it was something special that wasn't going to last, which seemed to have the effect of making her so much more aware of every aspect of it.

Oh, yeah…and knowing that it was safe because Nate wasn't pretending that there was any more to this than a 'friends with benefits' thing. He wasn't going to break her heart by dumping her in favour of someone who wanted to make babies with him. You couldn't dump someone that you weren't officially in any kind of relationship with anyway. And Nate already had the baby thing sorted. He was happy to be tackling the parent thing as a single dad. Even this afternoon, he'd been talking about the kind of woman he hoped to find as a live-in nanny.

*A slightly younger version of Shirley would be perfect, don't you think?*

If Alice had wanted to define what it was like to share intimacy with Nate, however, she would never have thought of using words that might describe what it was like *this* time. Because it had never been like this before.

So slow.

So tender, Alice could actually feel a lump forming in her throat as she tipped her head back to let Nate trail kisses down her neck, all the way to her breast. She had her fingers in his hair, cupping his head, but the only thing she was really aware of was the feeling of being…cherished.

Loved…

Weirdly, the level of heat from a powerful physical attraction was still there but it was being tempered with something that felt both incredibly soft but solid at the same time. Something real and dependable and still safe.

This was the difference between having sex and making love, wasn't it?

A tiny alarm bell rang somewhere in the back of her mind, but was it really something to worry about?

Alice couldn't begin to think about that right now. Not when Nate's hand was gliding over the curve of her hip and heading towards the part of her that was desperate for his touch.

Thinking could wait.

The only thing that mattered in this moment

was a sea of sensation that she would be happy to swim in for however long it was going to last.

And she was just as content to lie in Nate's arms when they were both limp with the relaxation that could only come in the wake of unbelievably good sex. Alice could feel her eyes drifting shut but she couldn't go to sleep like this. Having sex with Nate was one thing. Waking up with him was crossing a boundary that would make this more than what it was.

It wouldn't hurt to stay here for a few more minutes, though, would it? Just to have one of those lovely pillow-talk kind of chats? It didn't matter what they talked about, she just wanted to hear—and feel—the rumble of Nate's voice.

'I should have let Gareth cut the cord,' she said. 'Do you think he was disappointed?'

'We had rather a lot going on right then,' Nate responded. 'And I don't think he even noticed. He was too busy watching the miracle of their baby getting pinker with every breath he took. And so proud that they were giving him his father's name.'

'Have you thought of names for *your* baby?'

'Not really.' Nate sounded suddenly shy. 'It kind of felt too early. Like it might be tempting fate or something.'

Alice could hear what lay beneath his words. That desperate desire to be a father. To have a family of his own. She had the strongest urge to reassure him.

'It's not too soon,' she said. 'Simone's into the third trimester. Even if the baby did arrive early, she's going to have every chance of being absolutely fine.'

'I know. I just…worry a bit.'

'I know.' Alice turned her head just enough to let her lips touch his skin. An almost kiss that she hoped would tell Nate that she understood. That the fact that he cared enough about his baby to be worried was part of what was going to make him such a great dad. 'So…what's your mother's name?'

'Ruth. Bit old-fashioned now, isn't it?'

'It might be a lovely middle name. Any other family names you like?'

'I had an Aunt Winona. And my gran on my father's side was Daisy.'

'Oh…' Alice was smiling. 'I *love* Daisy.'

'You know what?'

'What?'

'I think I do, too.'

'Are you going to be at her birth?'

'I hope so,' Nate said. 'It will depend on how fast the labour is, of course. Who knows? Simone's had so much practice, she might end up having her at home before she gets anywhere near a hospital.'

Alice could feel his breath being released in a long sigh. 'I can't wait to hold her,' he said, very softly. 'I want to know that she's safely in the world and to let her know how much she's loved. That she's always going to be the most important person in the world to me.'

'You're going to be such a wonderful father,' Alice reminded him. 'Daisy is going to be a very lucky little girl.'

His arms tightened around her a little. 'Do you know anything about *your* father?' he asked.

'Not really. He went to the same school as my mum. They hooked up at some end-of-term party. When she told him she was pregnant, he said it wasn't a problem, it was easy enough to get abortions these days.' She swallowed hard. '*He* definitely didn't want me. I don't know why my mother didn't take his advice. Maybe she just left it too late...'

Nate was still holding her close. 'It's no wonder you grew up to spend your life caring for others,' he said. 'You knew too well what it was like to not be cared about, didn't you?'

'I guess.'

Her voice wobbled. Tucked into Nate's arm like this, with the warmth of his skin under her cheek and not having to make direct eye contact made it easy for words to fall out that she might never have otherwise spoken. She couldn't tell him about how she'd felt when she'd been holding baby Edward today—that, for a moment, she'd actually felt such a deep desire to be holding a baby of her own. She didn't want to remember how powerful that feeling had been. What she needed to do was to remind herself of the reason why she had decided so irrevocably that it couldn't be allowed to happen.

'I'd never forgive myself if I made someone feel like that,' she whispered. 'As if they had so little importance that the world would be a better place if they weren't in it.'

'Oh… *Alice…*' There was a catch in Nate's voice now. 'I hate that you ever felt like that.' He pulled in a slow breath. 'I want you to know that *my* world is an infinitely better place because you're in it.'

'Aww…that's probably the nicest thing anybody's ever said to me.'

'I mean it.' Nate pressed a kiss to her hair. 'If it wasn't for you, I'd still be living out of boxes and feeling like my life was a complete train wreck. Now I'm looking forward to a whole new future. With my daughter…with Daisy…'

Alice wasn't really listening to his soft words. She was still hearing him tell her that she was rocking his world. She could still hear that note in his voice when he'd said her name. *Alice…* As if his heart was breaking for her.

It would be so easy to fall in love with this man. She could feel it hovering around her like a mist. Or perhaps it was more like a magnetic force because she could feel herself being pulled into it.

The alarm bell was louder this time and the fact that it had sounded twice in such a short period of time meant that it couldn't be ignored.

This wasn't supposed to be happening.

She had to make sure it *didn't* happen.

Alice eased herself away from Nate's side. 'I'd better get going,' she said. 'Early start again tomorrow.'

'You could stay,' Nate said quietly. 'I've got a spare toothbrush somewhere.'

'Maybe another time.' Alice rolled away and got her feet onto the floor, reaching for the first item of her scattered clothing. Crossing that boundary was the complete opposite of what she needed to do right now.

She had to get out of this room. Out of Nate's house. She could have a peek in that adorable nursery as she went past to get to the stairs. She could remind herself that she'd always been adamant that she did not want to have a family. What had happened earlier today had been nothing more than hormones. Her body trying to make her take notice of the ticking of her biological clock.

She could also remind herself of what Nate had

said only minutes ago—that he couldn't wait to hold his daughter in his arms. To let her know that she would always be the most important person in his life.

Was Alice destined to never know what that might feel like, to be that important to someone? She'd missed out on it as a child. Was that what she'd been trying—and failing—to find in every relationship she'd had as an adult? To be enough. Just on her own. To know that she could make someone's world a better place, just by being in it. So much better that they didn't need anyone else in that innermost circle of their lives. They could simply be a couple, not a family.

Too much had happened today. It had pushed her even closer to Nate and she knew he was feeling it as well. The evidence had been there in every moment of their love-making. In Nate's invitation to cross that unspoken boundary.

They were turning into a couple.

What was waiting around the next corner? Would Nate start to hope that she might change her mind about motherhood? That she could step into the gap that he—and the baby—would have in their lives?

The thought sent a chill down her spine. She couldn't do that. Her grandmother had helped to ensure she would never change her mind. There was no getting away from the fact that she was her mother's daughter and there was only one way to be absolutely sure that history was not going to repeat itself.

For the sake of everyone involved, including a baby that wasn't even born yet, she needed to rein it in. Before someone got hurt.

There was no choice to be made here. It was going to happen anyway so it might as well be now.

It was time to back off.

# CHAPTER TEN

NATE STARED AT the phone in his hand.

He wanted to ring Alice. Not just text her. He wanted to hear her voice but he was hesitating. Because they'd only ever messaged each other and an actual phone call and conversation, especially late at night, felt like a boundary line.

Like staying a whole night with each other?

He'd made a mistake suggesting that the other night, hadn't he? It had been obvious that Alice wasn't feeling comfortable by the way she'd got dressed again so hurriedly—as if she was escaping.

But he was missing her. Missing her voice. Missing her touch even more. So much, it was almost a physical ache.

It would be well within the boundaries of friendship to ring and ask how her day had been today. To check in that she hadn't had to deal with any more cases as dramatic as that birth had been. But that wasn't why Nate wanted to talk to her.

He started tapping his screen.

Heard from Donna today, he texted. She and Nico are heading to the States to live. She wants a divorce.

A sad face emoji landed moments later along with a short message.

Are you ok?

Surprisingly, Nate *was* okay. It had been a very emotional exchange but amongst the swirls of regret and grief for a lost relationship, there was relief to be found. His marriage was definitively over after limping along for far too long. He and Donna could tidy up the mess they'd made of the recent years and get on with their lives. As Alice had said to him herself, not that long ago, nobody could live their best life if they were unhappy and he hadn't realised how miserable Donna had been for a long time. Nobody went looking for someone else to fall in love with if they were happy in their marriage, did they?

I knew it was coming, he responded. I'm thinking it might be time to tell Simone what's going on. She asked today if Donna was having phone problems because she hasn't had her messages picked up.

The silence seemed to stretch as he waited for the ping of a response.

That will give you a starting point to say something's changed. At least she knows how important this baby is to you now. Good luck! Keep me posted.

Nate blinked. He'd been hoping for a different response. A reason to put it off even longer? Advice on what to say?

*Support...?*

Yeah...he'd been counting on support from the only other person who knew what was going on in his life, and that message was leaving him feeling oddly...abandoned?

Good grief...where had *that* come from?

Will do, he messaged back. See you at work.

Not this week. Auckland friend's husband broke his big toe and she's persuaded me to take his place on a 3-day horse trek. Driving up to Napier tomorrow.

Nate was staring at his phone again. That unpleasant sensation of being rejected was growing in intensity and—added to that need to talk to her and the desire to be even closer than that—it could only mean one thing.

He was relying too much on Alice. Their friendship was becoming too important. He was, he realised, in danger of falling in love with her and that could only end badly. The warning signs had been there when she couldn't get away fast enough after that invitation to stay the night—as if they were a real couple.

How had he not been aware that they were drifting too close? That boundaries were beginning to feel as if they could be pushed? It was a good thing that Alice was going to be away for a few days. They needed a reset, here. Finding a way to tell Simone he was going to be a single parent was more than enough to cope with right now.

How stupid would it be to even be thinking about sailing into another relationship disaster? That was another pearl of wisdom Alice had shared once, wasn't it? That a relationship was never going to work if they weren't on the same page for the big things, like whether or not they wanted kids. He might be convinced that Alice was wrong about not wanting them but it might be something she would never be ready to admit.

Will do, he sent back. Have fun and don't fall off.

'I didn't fall off.'

Alice was beaming at Nate when he found her in the storeroom, restocking one of their kits before his next shift at Aratika started. She'd caught some sun on her days away, which had given her some new freckles on her nose. She looked proud of herself and very happy and…

And how had he never taken that much notice of how gorgeous she was? He'd been physically attracted to her, of course, but there was so much more to Alice Barlow. She had her life sorted, didn't she? Any partner she chose would have to be just as free. Just as adventurous. Just…totally different to how his life was going to be for the foreseeable future. A pang of regret came from nowhere, that Nate couldn't be that man.

'Was it fun?'

'*So* much fun. We covered farmland and stayed in shearers' quarters but there were the most beautiful forests to go through. And beaches! Have you ever galloped a horse through the waves on a totally deserted beach?'

'Can't say I have.'

'Try it sometime. Soon.'

Nate managed a chuckle. 'Like that night shift you said I needed to do before my life is totally taken over by a tiny human?'

'Absolutely. Three days on horseback would be even further out of reach.'

'I did a night shift. While you were away.'

'Really?' Alice reached up for a box of dressings but then she groaned loudly. 'I can't believe how stiff I am. I hadn't ridden for years and now every muscle in my body is hurting.'

'Sounds like you need some paracetamol. And a massage.'

*Oh*…imagine that. Some oil on his hands and Alice's skin beneath them…

Alice threw him a smile but didn't quite meet his eyes. 'Paracetamol's a good idea.' She took a couple of tablets from a bottle. 'I think I'm done here. Let's go and grab a coffee so I can wash these down.'

Nate picked up the backpack. Alice held the door to the room open. 'So how did it go?' she asked.

'The night shift? It was good. Only one call-out, to a car versus tree about an hour north. The night vision goggles were fun.'

'That wasn't what I meant.' Alice lowered her voice as they reached the main staircase that led up to the staff room. 'How did it go talking to Simone? About…you know…'

It was Nate's turn to avoid direct eye contact. He pretended a need to adjust his grip on the backpack straps. 'I haven't talked to her yet,' he admitted.

'Oh…'

Such a small word. It was a wonder it could pack such a punch that Nate could feel it in his gut hard enough to make him wince.

Was she disappointed in his lack of action?

He couldn't blame her. He was disappointed in

himself, to be honest, and he also had the horrible feeling that he was losing the control he thought he'd had regained over his life. Could he admit that he'd been missing Alice?

A lot?

That he'd been waiting for her return because he really wanted to talk to her? After several dead-end attempts at a written confession, explanation and sincere apology, he was worried that it might make things worse to handle something like this via the impersonal route of a text message or email. A phone connection was quite likely to be patchy, however, and quite possibly get cut off and that could leave things unsaid and hanging awkwardly. It felt like he was between a rock and a hard place and the only person he could talk to about it was Alice but now wasn't the time to try. Andy was coming into the hangar, heading their way.

'Good to see we've got the Dream Team on board today,' he said cheerfully. 'Hasn't been the same without you two.'

Alice had to wonder, as the day wore on, whether Andy was still so pleased with his medical crew for the shift.

She was finding the atmosphere reminiscent of what it had been like to work with Nate when she knew about his marriage falling apart but had no idea of the real turmoil going on in his life, and she was uncomfortably aware that this might be due to her decision to try and create a safer distance between them. Maybe she was trying too hard and there was a danger that she was going to lose what she most wanted to keep—that level of friendship and that trust, both personal and professional—but what else could she do?

This *was* hard.

The flip side of the coin that the ease of falling in love with Nate would have been.

It was, in fact, a lot harder than Alice had expected it to be, but that only made her more determined to succeed. For both their sakes.

And maybe this new tension was due more to the fact that he still hadn't told Simone about Donna? It was perfectly understandable that it was proving a difficult thing for him to do. He'd been worried all along that Simone might be shocked that the baby she was carrying was going to be raised by a single parent but, having made that spur-of-the-moment decision to use the accidental deception that was available when Simone had arrived on the doorstep so unexpectedly, he'd inadvertently given her another reason she might not consider him an ideal parent, hadn't he?

He'd lied to her. He'd let her think that Alice was Donna.

She'd played her part in that deception. She could still remember that look in Nate's eyes and an unspoken plea that was coming straight from his heart that she couldn't possibly refuse.

*Please...don't say anything. Can we pretend? It's only for an hour...*

She could remember the touch of his hand, too. That sizzle of electricity that should have been all the warning she needed that she was in danger of falling in love with Nathaniel Madden.

Did she heed that warning?

Ha! She'd practically run past any red flags that might have been waving. She'd kissed him, for heaven's sake. She'd convinced herself that she'd be helping Nate even more by letting Simone see them kissing, like happily married parents-to-be.

Alice sighed. Even thinking about that kiss was like giving her body, and her heart, permission to relive exactly what it had been like to kiss Nate that first time and open a door to so much more. To mix in the pang of longing to experience it again. Longing that was strong enough to feel like a *need*.

Yeah...if things became difficult, she would have to shoulder her fair share of the blame.

She knew how devastating it would be for Nate if things became really difficult, so it was hardly surprising that this palpable tension was there.

* * *

Thank goodness it turned out to be one of those days where it was a bonus to find time to have a bathroom break. Alice hoped it was as easy for Nate as it was for her to forget about anything personal as they treated and transported patients. Half the morning was taken up with their first call to a remote farm, where a young man had managed to roll his ATV down a bank and had fractured his pelvis, judging by the level of pain he was in and the instability of what was normally a rigid, bony structure.

It was an injury that carried the possibility of life-threatening internal bleeding and required the air ambulance team's full focus. They got IV access and provided strong pain relief but needed extra help from the local volunteer fire brigade to get their patient out from under the heavy, four-wheeled bike without making his injury worse. It was only then that they could apply the pelvic binder that would help tamponade any bleeding and continue the intensive monitoring for signs of shock as they got him to the emergency department of The General.

There was a quick turnaround after the handover as they were dispatched to back up another helicopter at a major scene where a car had collected more than one rider in a motorbike club's road trip. Lunch was sandwiches from a cafeteria in the hospital foyer and time on-base was only long enough to restock the kits and refuel the aircraft.

The next job was more sedate—simply a transfer from a rural hospital for a patient who had suffered a heart attack that was severe enough for her to need to be in a catheter laboratory for angioplasty within a window of time that could prevent ongoing cardiac damage. It was as they arrived back on base that Nate got a text message on his phone. His expression, as he read it, made Alice's heart sink.

'It's Simone,' he said. 'Her midwife says her blood pressure is too high. She's going to take her into Invercargill Hospital as soon as Olly gets home from the farm he's working on, so he can look after the kids.'

'Did she say what her blood pressure was?'

'I'll ask.' Nate texted swiftly and didn't look up as he waited for a response. 'One-fifty over ninety-five.' His tone was grim. 'That's pre-eclampsia territory.'

Alice bit her lip. Pre-eclampsia could morph into full-blown eclampsia the moment a seizure occurred and that was an obstetric emergency for both the mother and baby. It could cause lack of oxygen during seizures or a placental abruption. There was a risk of stroke or organ failure and, in a worst-case scenario, it could be fatal.

Nate was still focussed on his phone. 'She says she hasn't got any visual disturbances but she does have a headache and her ankles are swollen. She'll let me know more when she's been seen at the hospital.'

It was just as well there were no further callouts that afternoon. Even with the best of professional intentions it would have been a challenge to shut this down. If further tests confirmed that Simone did have pre-eclampsia, she would have to be admitted to hospital for continuous monitoring and medications to try and lower her blood pressure, prevent seizures and prolong the pregnancy. Delivery was the only cure, however, and it would have to happen with any signs of danger to either mother or baby, regardless of dates.

Simone was barely into her third trimester. Nate's precious baby would be very premature and that could add a whole new layer to the complications in his life. Alice's heart was aching for him as she watched him pacing the base, his phone in his hand, glancing at the screen frequently. Sometimes he was staring at it as if he was willing it to ring or sound an alert for a message.

In the end it did ring. Alice could see Nate walking outside, near the helicopter, making sure the call was private. She went down to meet him when he came back into the hangar. It was time they should be heading off shift, anyway.

'She's had blood tests and an ultrasound,' Nate told her. 'The baby's fine. They've got her on continuous CTG monitoring and she's on bed rest. They're going to keep her in for observation for the next twenty-four hours.'

Alice nodded. 'That's good. They haven't confirmed pre-eclampsia, then?'

'Not yet.'

The shadows in Nate's eyes were haunting. It was all Alice could do not to offer him a hug.

'You want to get down there, don't you?'

A single nod from Nate. 'I've been checking flights. I've got a day off tomorrow and I could get there by mid-morning. They should know how serious this is by then.'

Alice mirrored his nod. She wanted to reassure him but how? She would go home with him tonight just to be there for him but that didn't feel like enough.

She cared about this man. Too much, maybe, but that was beside the point right now. She had to *do* something.

'If we let Don know what's going on, I know he'd get someone in to cover for me,' she said quietly. 'Would you like me to come with you? To see Simone?'

Alice could see the softening in his eyes that

was a kind of melting. She could *feel* it happening in her own heart.

'Yes,' he whispered. '*Please…*'

# CHAPTER ELEVEN

'OH, MY GOODNESS…' Simone was astonished to see Nate and Alice come into her room the next morning. 'You've come all this way! *Both* of you…'

'We were worried about you,' Nate said. 'I'm sorry we couldn't get here any sooner. I rang a couple of times overnight but all they would tell me was that you were sleeping comfortably.'

'I feel fine,' Simone said. 'Just a bit of a headache, that's all. I'm sure they're going to let me go back home today. They're just waiting to see what the results of the latest blood tests are, I think. I'm sorry to have given you such a fright. Are you okay, Donna?'

Alice swallowed hard. She'd known this would be the hardest part of supporting Nate through this, but she had no choice but to continue the pretence of being his wife. They'd both agreed that today was not the time for honesty. Upsetting someone whose blood pressure was already too high would be an irresponsible thing to do.

Unacceptable from both a professional and personal standpoint.

'We'll both be fine, too,' she said. 'Once we know that *you're* okay. And please, just say if there's anything we can do to help. We've got flights booked back for this afternoon but they can be changed if we need to.'

Simone shook her head. 'Olly's got everything sorted with the kids. I think he loves an opportunity to show off what a great dad he is. He's going to bring them all in for the ride this afternoon, either to visit me or take me home.' She smiled. 'You'd be welcome to come for dinner, if you want to rent a car and stay the night. I'd love you to meet the kids and see where we live.'

Alice didn't know how to respond to the invitation. She turned to Nate but he seemed to be focussed on the screen of the cardiotocography machine although it looked reassuringly normal. The line for the transducer measuring contractions was completely flat and the fetal heart rate was a healthy, rapid blip of about a hundred and forty beats a minute.

They were both saved from having to say anything by the arrival of the medical team doing their ward round. They stepped back out of the way as the small group of doctors, a nurse and a midwife surrounded Simone's bed.

The consultant opened Simone's notes. 'Latest

blood results are looking good,' she said. 'Your kidney and liver function is fine and your platelets are normal. How's that headache?'

'Not too bad.'

'On the pain scale of one to ten?'

'Still only about two. It's just a nuisance, that's all.'

'Let's have a look at that swelling in your ankles.'

A nurse lifted the covers of Simone's bed to reveal that the swelling had decreased overnight.

'Amazing what staying off your feet for a while can do,' Simone said. 'My blood pressure's down a bit, too, isn't it?'

A junior doctor picked up the chart on the end of the bed. 'Last reading was one-forty over ninety,' he said.

'Still a bit high,' the consultant told Simone. 'But it's stable and not enough to warrant starting medication at the moment. Try and stay off your feet more, if you can. We're going to give you an easy-to-use automatic cuff so you can take your blood pressure daily at home and we'll be asking your midwife to check on you more often. We're happy that this is gestational hypertension and not pre-eclampsia but we also want you to come back here immediately if you notice any new symptoms, like visual disturbances, abdominal pain or a reduction in baby's movements.'

She nodded at Nate and Alice as she turned back to the door. Had she assumed they were family members or simply visitors?

'These are the baby's parents,' Simone told her. 'Nate's a doctor, too. From Wellington.'

Nate put his hand out. 'Nate Madden,' he said as she accepted the handshake. 'Nice to meet you.'

'I'm Maria. I've delivered three of Simone's babies in the last few years and we're happy to support her in this surrogacy.'

She turned to Alice with a friendly smile. 'You've come a long way. I'm Maria,' she repeated as they shook hands. 'Good to meet you.'

'And you.' Alice smiled back. 'I'm Alice.'

Oh, *no*... The minute her name left her lips and Alice realised what her automatic reaction had revealed, she cringed inwardly and her smile vanished. She could feel the atmosphere in the room changing around her.

Maria hadn't noticed. She was still smiling. 'You'll both be happy to know that the results of the ultrasound we did yesterday are all on track. Normal growth, no problems with the amniotic fluid volume or the blood flow through the umbilical artery. Baby's doing well.'

'That's great news.' But Nate's voice sounded tight.

'I'll be back soon,' the midwife told Simone as

she turned to leave. 'I'll bring the blood pressure cuff and teach you how to use it.'

Simone nodded but said nothing.

Within seconds, the medical staff had moved on to their next patient and it was just the three of them in the room again. Alice could feel Simone's stare but she was transfixed by the expression on Nate's face.

He looked as though she'd just betrayed him. She felt like she'd betrayed him and she wished the floor would just open up and swallow her. She'd hurt Nate but she could feel the pain and it was…unbearable.

A single word, from Simone, fell into the silence in a tone of both confusion and accusation.

*'Alice…?'*

'I can explain.'

Now that the initial shock was wearing off, Nate felt a wash of something like relief. 'I've been wanting to tell you for a long time but—'

'Tell me *what*?' Simone demanded. 'That your wife has changed her name? Wait…' Her gaze swerved to Alice. 'You're *not* Donna, are you?'

'No.' Alice had to stop herself from looking at Nate. 'I'm sorry,' she added. 'It just kind of happened. When you turned up that day and assumed I was Donna.'

Simone was shaking her head. 'Of course I

did. You were in Nate's house. You were so obviously a…a *couple—*'

'No…' It was Nate who interrupted this time. 'We were just friends.' His sigh was resigned. He couldn't keep lying. He should never have let this happen in the first place. 'Then…'

Simone was rubbing her forehead and Nate's heart fell even further. Was her headache getting worse? Had he been justified in wanting to keep up the pretence to avoid exacerbating what could still be a complication in this pregnancy?

'How stupid could I have been?' Simone muttered. 'If I hadn't been so excited about sharing the video of that scan with you, I would have paid more attention. I knew that your wife looked different from her photos. I just thought it was because she wasn't expecting visitors and didn't have any makeup on or something.' Her head jerked up. 'Where *is* Donna?'

'She's gone. She's been in Italy and is now moving to the United States.'

'I'm not surprised.' Simone sounded disgusted. 'How long has this been going on?' Simone looked from Nate to Alice and back again. 'This…*affair*?'

'Please…' Nate moved closer. 'Let me explain.'

'Um…' Alice sounded uncertain. 'Would it be better if I left?'

Nate hated that he'd created this situation. He'd

made Alice complicit in a deception that might have happened unintentionally but he'd chosen to prolong it. He couldn't blame her for having used her own name when she introduced herself to Maria. This might be a very difficult situation but it wasn't Alice's fault. He had to take the blame and try and put this right.

'If might be better,' he agreed. 'This is between me and Simone and I need to tell her everything.'

The whole story. About Donna walking away from the prospect of bringing up a child when she wasn't the biological mother. Of walking away from being his wife. About the affair she was having that he hadn't known about. Of how Alice had been helping him to try and show her how committed he was to being the best father to his baby. *His* baby…

'I'll meet you at the airport, then,' Alice said quietly.

It was an hour later that Nate arrived back at the airport. He spotted Alice almost instantly, sitting on the far side of the waiting area. Even from this distance he could see that she'd been anxiously watching for him.

'I'm *so* sorry,' she said as soon as he got close enough. 'I can't believe I did that. I just…wasn't thinking.'

'It's not your fault.' Nate tried to smile but his

lips wouldn't cooperate. 'I was the one who let it happen in the first place. I could have just said you were a friend and none of this would have happened.'

He wanted to sound reassuring but it was too difficult. He'd known all along that precisely this would have happened. His entire future had been hanging on that conversation with Simone that he had put off for far too long.

Nate was totally drained.

And afraid.

'Is Simone okay?' Alice asked.

'Physically? Yes. She's upset but it hasn't made any difference to her blood pressure.'

Alice was biting her lip. 'What did she say?'

'That she needs to talk to Olly about it. That she needs time to think about it.' Nate turned away. 'Have you checked in?'

'Yes.'

He nodded. That meant Alice already had a seat so it was unlikely they would be seated together and that was probably a good thing.

There really wasn't anything more to say at the moment, was there?

He had given his evidence to the best of his ability and now the jury was out.

There was nothing either of them could do other than wait for the verdict to arrive.

# CHAPTER TWELVE

THE WAITING WAS the worst.

Alice texted Nate two days later but he hadn't had any communication from Simone at that point. He said he'd let her know when he heard something.

So she kept waiting and resisted the urge to find another reason to make contact.

It wasn't what she wanted to do. What she wanted was to turn up on Nate's doorstep. To walk into his house and…

And what?

Hope that he would pull her into his arms and tell her that everything was going to be okay? That he'd fallen in love with her and couldn't live without her? That she was just as important to him as the baby?

No…all she really wanted to do was to hold him in *her* arms. To comfort him. To tell him again how sorry she was. To let him know how much she cared about him, even if she couldn't say it aloud because it might well be the last thing he wanted to hear when his life had got even more complicated.

But neither of those scenarios were going to happen, were they?

Nate had made it very clear, when he'd opened up to her in the first place, that his unborn baby was the most important thing in his life, and his ability to be a father to that baby was in jeopardy. While Alice knew that it really wasn't her fault that this had happened, that didn't stop her feeling responsible. She'd been well-trained, after all, to know that her presence in someone's life was enough to be a problem. That just her existence could diminish someone else's happiness.

Perhaps the best thing to do was to stay well clear of Nate.

She also thought he might be deliberately avoiding her, giving that he wasn't even texting, so she wasn't really expecting to see him turn up for his next rostered shift at Aratika but there he was, already in the staff room when she arrived, with Shirley fussing over him, trying to tempt him to accept one of her delicious bacon rolls.

'Or at least an egg on toast? You look like you're losing weight.' Shirley tutted. 'You're not looking after yourself well enough, are you?' With a sigh, she gave up. 'What's that book you've got? It looks very old.'

'It's *The Hobbit*.' Nate showed her the battered

green cover of the book that he'd found in that second-hand bookshop. 'I started reading it last night and I couldn't put it down. Thought it would make a change from medical journals if we get time on base today.'

He did look tired, Alice thought. The lines around his eyes were deeper and his smile looked like it was taking considerable effort. How much sleep was he getting? Had he been up half the night reading to try and distract himself? Had he *still* not heard back from Simone?

As if he'd caught her thought, Nate glanced up and gave a clear message with a subtle shake of his head. There was no news.

Andy and Nick broke off the conversation they were having as Don came out of the operations room.

'Your pagers are about to go off,' he told the crew. 'Car versus cyclist on the Paekākāriki Hill road. Sounds like someone came down the off-ramp like there was no tomorrow. According to the first responder it looks like a partial amputation with a fracture/dislocation of an ankle. They've only got methoxyflurane as an analgesic and it's not doing much to help the poor guy.'

Pagers sounding drowned out his voice but the crew were already moving. Weather was not an issue with a cloudless sky and little wind, Andy and Nick had already done the pre-flight checks on the helicopter and any further information could be relayed during the time it took them to get airborne and over the hills to the west coast.

Alice was grateful for the call. It had to be better for both herself and Nate to be busy and working. Sitting around the base, sneaking glances at him and worrying about his state of mind would make for a very long and miserable day.

They were back to square one and Alice was beginning to wonder if this was going to affect Nate's ability to do his job effectively. It felt like a lower dip in the rollercoaster of their professional and personal relationship, however, because she'd learned what it was like to be close to him. To share his secrets and know what hopes and fears he had for his future. She knew what it was like to be really close, in fact, and that made this so much more personal. What was bothering Nate mattered to her as well.

It mattered a lot.

They could see traffic banking up below them in both directions as they neared the scene. Emergency vehicles with their beacons flashing made it easy to spot their target. An ambulance, fire trucks and police cars had responded and a tow-truck was trying to weave through the snarled traffic. Police officers had blocked off part of the adjoining state highway to give the helicopter a safe landing area not far from the group of people clustered around the accident victim.

The local first responders looked very relieved to see expert help arriving and it was easy to see why as Alice and Nate crouched beside a young man who was screaming with pain. His whole ankle joint was visible, the foot hanging on an angle below, looking very pale and completely lifeless.

'Do you know his name?' Nate asked the first responder.

'Peter.'

Nate crouched. 'Peter? Can you hear me? My name's Nate and I'm a doctor. We're going to get on top of that pain for you, okay?'

Their patient gave him an agonised glance but just groaned in response.

Alice was right beside him, unzipping the pack. Nick was setting down an oxygen cylinder near Peter's head.

'Want O2 on?'

'Yes, thanks. Let's get some leads on and a BP, too. Peter?' He leaned closer. 'I'm going to put an IV line in your arm so we can give you some stronger pain relief. Is that okay?'

Peter was sucking on the mouthpiece of the Penthrox inhaler but managed to nod this time, which rang an alarm bell for Alice. Peter might have been wearing a helmet but, with a mechanism of injury like this, the head and neck could well be involved and the distraction of the pain he was in from his ankle, any signs or symptoms could be buried.

'Try and keep your head as still as you can for the moment,' she told him.

'Blood pressure's one-fifty over ninety,' Nick reported as Alice handed Nate the Luer plug to attach to the end of the cannula. 'Heart rate one-twenty. Resps twenty-four.'

Alice leaned down so Peter could hear her over the reverse beeping signal of a tow-truck backing in to hook up the car that had been involved in this incident. 'Are you allergic to anything that you know of, Peter?'

'No…'

His groan became a crescendo into another scream. Alice gripped his shoulder. 'Hang in there, Peter. The doctor's drawing up some drugs right now that are going to take that pain away.'

She assumed he would be using ketamine because it was the most potent analgesic and sedative they had available and something powerful was going to be needed to align this fracture. The wound was heavily contaminated so it would also need irrigation with saline before sterile wound dressings and immobilisation in a splint.

Alice saw Nate looking around them before he

injected the drug and she knew he was worried about how busy the scene was. Ketamine was the ideal drug to use in this situation but it did have the potential to cause hallucinations and severe agitation in some patients, and there was a lot of stimulation around them that could trigger a reaction. Flashing lights were very close, horns were blaring from irate drivers who were fed up with being caught in a traffic jam because there was a helicopter sitting in the middle of the road, people were shouting and a siren from another emergency vehicle arriving could be heard.

Nate caught Alice's gaze and gave his head a slight shake. There wasn't much they could do to try and make things calmer and quieter but Alice put her face close to Peter's and kept talking to him. Reassurance and distraction could be helpful as well.

'You're doing really well, Peter,' she told him. 'We're going to give you some medication now so we can get your leg sorted and then we'll put you in the helicopter and get you to hospital. Have you ever been in a helicopter before?'

Peter's eyes were open and he was staring up at her. When Alice saw the involuntary movements as his eyes flicked from side to side, she knew that Nate had administered the ketamine and it was taking effect.

Nate moved Peter's leg gently to check the level of sedation.

'All good?' he asked.

Peter's eyes were still open but he wasn't showing any sign of being aware of what was going on or experiencing any pain.

'All good,' Alice responded.

'Can I get you to support the leg above the ankle, please? I'm going to put some longitudinal traction on the foot to get the joint back in. Nick, keep an eye on his breathing and sedation level.'

They didn't need their crewman to warn that there was a problem as the sedative effects of the ketamine began to wear off. Peter suddenly began struggling to sit up. He was ripping the oxygen mask from his face and shouting.

'Get them away…we're going to get trampled…'

Nick put his hands on Peter's shoulders to reassure him and push him gently back to a lying position.

'Watch his neck,' Nate snapped. 'C-spine isn't cleared yet.'

'It's all right, Peter. Nothing's going to trample us.' Alice tried to catch hold of his hands but he swung his arm towards her and she fell backwards as the blow connected to her cheek.

She heard Nate swear under his breath. She rolled on her side and pushed herself upright again, ignoring the stinging of the side of her face and the metallic taste of blood in her mouth. Nate was injecting more medication into the IV line as Nick held Peter's body in a tight hug.

'Midazolam?' she queried.

'Luckily I had some drawn up, just in case.' His gaze flicked sideways. 'Are you hurt?'

Alice touched the back of her hand to her lip to wipe away any blood that might be obvious. 'I'm fine.'

'He's settling,' Nick said, lowering Peter to the ground again.

'Let's get this dressed and securely splinted, then.' But Nate's gaze was searching Alice's face as she reached for some large, sterile dressings.

'I'm fine,' she repeated, more firmly. 'Forget about me.'

Nate had to do that, at least for now, but he could see that Alice had a cut on her lip and a red mark on her cheek and his mind was demanding to replay the moment she'd been struck and turn that spear of empathetic pain in his own gut into something solid and heavy. It was harder than it had ever been before to bury a personal reaction and do what had to be done.

Which was a rapid but thorough secondary survey now that the overwhelming distraction of the ankle injury had been dealt with. The steps of the head-to-toe sweep might be so well-practised for Nate that the process was automatic but this still required a level of focus that would ensure nothing got missed.

Like CSF fluid leaking from an ear that could indicate a skull fracture, perhaps. Reduced breath sounds, which could be a symptom of a serious chest injury or abdominal signs of internal bleeding. Another set of vital signs needed to be recorded, medication topped up and then they would be ready to secure Peter to the stretcher and get him into the helicopter for transport. The whole crew was kept busy and it wasn't until they had completed their handover in the trauma resuscitation room of the emergency department that Nate let himself take a more searching look at Alice's face.

Her cheek still looked red and her lip was swelling now.

'You need to get your lip checked out. And your cheek.'

Alice shook her head. 'It's nothing,' she muttered, not looking up from the paperwork she was completing.

Nate went to get some ice from the staffroom freezer and wrapped it in a gauze dressing pad.

'Here…' He handed her the cold pack. 'Keep this on your face for a while. I'll look after the stretcher.'

What he really wanted to do was hold her face between his hands and examine it properly. To touch her lip and make sure there wasn't a hidden cut deep enough to need stitches.

But Alice had made it obvious she wouldn't welcome that kind of attention. They'd barely spoken, in fact, since that awful moment in Simone's room when she'd suggested it would be better if she wasn't there. They hadn't been seated together on the plane and Alice had been as determined to escape the airport when they got back to Wellington as she had been to leave his bedroom the last time they'd slept together.

And maybe that would turn out to *actually* be the last time they were ever that close.

The distance had been growing ever since that night but Nate was doing his best to convince himself that this had been inevitable. That Alice had only ever been interested in something temporary and without any kind of strings.

With the horrible tension since Simone had learned the truth about their deception, he had even wondered whether it might help her decision-making if he could tell her that what she saw as an 'affair' with Alice was over. That he was not going to let anything other than his child have a claim on his attention for the foreseeable future.

Even that he was prepared to sacrifice a friendship that he knew *was* significant? Alice might have told him to forget about her but he knew, beyond any shadow of doubt, that was never going to happen.

The cold pack helped a lot.

Alice checked her lip in the bathroom mirror when they got back to base and she knew that the cut was small enough to heal easily on its own.

As she'd had to tell Nate more than once, she *was* fine.

Physically, anyway.

The fact that Nate had cared enough to make the ice pack for her wasn't helping her emotional state, though.

She hated this distance between them. She was missing him so much it hurt, dammit, and it didn't feel like it was going to wear off anytime soon.

Alice turned away from the mirror. Surely there was some way they could at least salvage the friendship they'd discovered before they'd allowed the attraction between them to make things complicated? She knew Nate was on tenterhooks waiting to hear from Simone and she knew how incredibly important this was to him.

He needed a friend right now more than he had when she'd first stepped up and pushed herself into his personal life. Alice gave the door a rather determined push and headed towards the staff room. She was just as determined to let Nate know that she was still in his corner and that a real friendship—like theirs—could survive anything if they both wanted it to.

She didn't get to say anything, however.

She found Nate standing by the floor-to-ceiling windows that made up the wall in this central, third-floor office area of the Aratika Rescue Base. The view was spectacular. Wellington Harbour straight ahead, the distinctive central city skyline a background on one side and rugged, forest-covered hills on the other. Directly below was the helipad but Nate wasn't watching Andy as he walked around his beloved yellow helicopter, possibly looking for a smudge of dust he could brush off.

Nate was, instead, looking at the screen of his phone. He looked up as Alice got close that the look in his eyes made her breath catch.

She didn't need to ask if it was a message from Simone. Nate handed her his phone and she could see that the communication was an email.

Dear Nate,
Thank you for your patience. Olly and I had a lot to talk and think about after this unexpected development in our surrogacy journey and we also decided that we should seek some legal advice.

As I'm sure you know, under NZ law, the woman who gives birth to a baby is the legal mother, regardless of any lack of genetic relationship. You will also be aware that the intended parents must apply for an adoption order and that this requires the surrogate (and her partner) to consent to the adoption. Without this consent, the adoption cannot proceed.

Alice couldn't breathe. She knew what was coming.

I'm very sorry, Nate, but Olly and I feel very strongly that, as a loving and complete family, we can offer this baby a better future than you will be able to.

The screen went blank but Alice didn't want to tap it back into life. She'd seen enough. She handed Nate his phone. She could feel tears gathering in her eyes as she met his gaze, but it still felt like she couldn't breathe and that meant she couldn't say anything, either.

Even if she'd been able to find the words…

The only thing she could do was to open her arms. To offer the comfort of a hug.

For one long horrible moment, Alice thought that Nate was going to refuse. That he would shake his head and turn away. It was quite understandable that he might want to be alone to deal with what had to be an unthinkable pain but…

But it would break Alice's heart.

Because this was how much she loved Nate. She could feel his pain as if it was her own and the need to offer comfort and support was so big it was filling her, body and soul.

And, in a moment that Alice would remember for the rest of her life, Nate didn't refuse. He not only stepped into her arms, he wrapped his around her and held her so tightly she could almost believe that he needed this physical contact as much as she did.

That he needed *her*?

But, what Nate did refuse, moments later, was her offer to go home with him so that he wasn't alone.

'No.' The word had a finality that seemed to echo around Alice. 'Thanks, but I'm going to go and see my solicitor. He's a friend so he won't mind talking to me away from work.'

'Call me when you can,' she said. 'Let me know if there's anything I can do to help.'

That wry smile nearly undid her.

'Thank you,' he said quietly, 'but you've already done more than enough. I shouldn't have involved you in this at all. I'm sorry, Alice. This is my problem. And it's up to me to find a way to fix it.'

# CHAPTER THIRTEEN

SHE HAD DONE 'more than enough.'

There was no way Alice couldn't pick up her fair share of the blame for this new challenge that Nate was facing.

He rang her that evening.

'It's not good news,' he said, without preamble. 'My solicitor, Rob, was straight with me and he said that it would be an uphill battle to persuade a family court to override the birth mother's rights.'

'But you're the father.' Alice was shocked. This was so unfair. 'You're the person who chose to create this baby—the only person here that's got a genetic connection.'

'Rob said I'd have to prove that there were serious concerns about the child's welfare so that I could go for a guardianship or custody.' He sounded even more tired than he'd looked this morning. 'I know that Simone and Olly are amazing parents, so that would be dishonest. I couldn't do that. It was a lack of honesty that's brought this to where it is and…it's not me.'

'I know,' Alice whispered. 'I knew that all along. I also knew that you had the best intentions in the world.'

There was a huff of sound that could have been an equal mix of laughter and a sob.

'Isn't that what the road to hell is paved with?'

Alice closed her eyes. What could she say?

'Rob said the best way to resolve this is to negotiate with Simone and Olly,' Nate said, into the silence. 'I just need to decide what the best way to go about that is. Wish me luck.'

'Of course I do. You know that.'

'I do.' Alice could hear Nate drawing in a deep breath, as if he wanted to say something else but, judging by the final tone of his next words, it seemed that he had changed his mind. 'Catch you later, Alice.'

There was no point trying to sleep yet, Alice decided later that evening. And she might end up missing Nate even more acutely if she was lying there in her bed, wide awake.

She wasn't hungry and she didn't want the noise of either a movie or music that might have distracted her. She decided to do some housework, instead, but the first thing she picked up to put back into the cupboard under the stairs was that box of wool that had been sitting beside the end of her couch ever since she'd made that pair of booties for Nate's baby.

She found herself sinking onto the couch, with that soft ball of pale yellow wool in her hands and, suddenly, knitting something seemed like the perfect distraction from the thoughts and emotions that were as tangled as some of the wool at the bottom of this box. The book of baby patterns was still on top of the box, along with the needles, and it didn't seem like a stupid idea to use them. She could use the rest of this yellow wool to knit a tiny hat. Maybe she could post it to Simone with a note of apology for her part in complicating what had been supposed to be a wonderful gift of creating a family for others.

It was soothing to focus on how many stitches to cast on and then follow the instructions to the lacy pattern for a sweet baby bonnet. For a while, even, Alice forgot that she was making an item of clothing for a newborn baby but, as the shape began to emerge, she found herself remembering the birth of Nicole's baby.

Or rather, the way she'd felt when she'd been holding that baby boy in her own arms.

And, this time, that surge of yearning was so strong, her needles stilled and she rested her hands in her lap.

Was this how Nate felt when he thought about the baby he wanted so much? When all he wanted to do was to hold his daughter and let her know how loved she was?

No…it had to be far worse for him. This was just the concept of a baby that was making Alice feel like this.

Nate's baby was *real*. She already existed. She was growing and she would be born and taking her first breaths in the very near future.

Alice barely noticed the tears trickling slowly down her face. She wanted Nate to be holding his baby as she took those first breaths.

She wanted to hold her *own* baby one day. To love her the way a baby should be loved. The way Nate would love his baby if he was allowed to.

The way every baby should be loved?

This flood of emotion couldn't be attributed simply to hormones or a biological clock. Alice could see that it had been there forever. Deeply locked away in order to dodge the painful memories that were inextricably linked to her own mother. But this was different. This flood was washing away the walls that had kept it locked up. She could see it for what it was. A childhood fear.

She wasn't a child now.

She knew how much love she was capable of giving. To a baby. To the father of that baby. And it mattered.

*She* mattered.

*I want you to know that my world is an infinitely better place because you're in it...*

Dear Lord…that emotional flood was washing away the final lumps of rubble that she'd believed had been keeping her safe all her life.

What was being left behind was the love she had for Nate. And for the little girl who should be called Daisy and be brought up with the father who loved her to the moon and back.

What was happening to Nate wasn't fair. It wasn't right.

She *had* to try and find some way to help fix this.

It was a day off for Nate but he was making a quick visit to the Aratika Rescue Base because he'd left something behind when he'd left yesterday.

He'd been so shocked by that email from Simone that he hadn't even thought to go back to the staff room and collect his book. He'd only remembered where it was, in fact, in the early hours of this morning, when he'd needed something to distract himself from the dark space his thoughts were trying to lure him into, and what better way to find a rock to cling to than to remind himself of his own father. It had been a real surprise to find he could almost hear his dad's voice in his head when he was reading *The Hobbit* but there was comfort to be found in that.

And Nate had never been in quite this need of comfort. He'd felt lost when his life seemed to be falling apart and he had no idea how he was going to cope with a new home to settle into and fatherhood just around the corner. But now…he felt broken. The dream he'd had of his own future had been well and truly shattered with not even a glimpse of a possible solution to be found yet.

The helicopters were on the ground when he arrived. He could see Andy standing in the sunshine, having a yarn with one of the other pilots. The back doors of the ambulance were open and it looked like the paramedic crew were doing a check of all the gear that was kept on board, in the overhead lockers and other storage areas.

There would be other staff members inside the building but Nate wasn't sure he wanted to be sociable enough to return greetings and field any jokes about how he couldn't stay away from the place. Alice would be on duty today and he didn't want to see the concern that would be in her eyes, because that would make it harder to try and stay in control. And what if Shirley was in the staff room today? One look at his face and she'd probably be wrapping her arms around him and offering him some of her home baking and that could well be his undoing.

Maybe he should go and have a quiet word with Andy and ask him to pop upstairs and collect the book? As he walked into the hangar, however, Nate's glance caught the spiral staircase and he remembered the door at the top and the corridor that led to the central hub of the base with the staff room and offices. Nobody would be using the on-call bedrooms during the day and, if he went up that way, he could open the door far enough to see how crowded the area was and whether he could face it. If he couldn't, he'd go and talk to Andy.

He hadn't factored in how he would feel going up these steel stairs and quietly opening the door that led into the corridor, mind you. Oh, man… the memories of the way that physical attraction between himself and Alice had ignited with such force that neither of them could resist giving in to it right then and there…

He'd never experienced a physical connection to anybody like that, including the woman he'd married, and he doubted that he would ever find it again. The way it had felt as if they'd always known each other. As if their bodies were made for each other. Sex had never felt wilder or more exciting but oddly, it had never felt that safe, either.

Nate was halfway along the corridor, sinking into emotions rather than coherent thoughts, when he heard a voice that stopped him in his tracks.

*Alice?*

What on earth was she doing here?

In one of the on-call rooms. The one just ahead of him, its door ajar.

'I'm in a completely private area,' he heard Alice say. 'So no one will be able to hear and I'm on my lunch break, so I won't be called out unless it's a real emergency.'

Nate was turning. He needed to retrace his steps. Alice was trying to make a very private call and he didn't want her to know he was here.

Alice cleared her throat as he was about to move. 'Thank you so much for this. I hope you didn't go into town just so we could get a good enough reception for a video call.'

'It's okay. I had to come in for a midwife appointment, anyway.'

Nate froze. He knew that voice. Alice was talking to *Simone*. There was no way he could move now. He might not be a part of this conversation but it could only be *about* him. He had to know what the hell was going on. Simone didn't sound that happy. Was Alice about to do something that might make it even less likely that he could somehow negotiate a change of heart from his surrogate?

'Olly said it was only fair,' Simone added. 'I

listened to what Nate had to say, so I should listen to you. So, shoot…what is it that you're so desperate to tell me?'

'Oh…' It sounded like Alice didn't know where to start. 'I just think there are some things you probably don't know about and maybe what you do know isn't the whole story.'

'Like what?'

'Like how committed Nate is to being a father. To having a family. I've been working with him for over a year but I've only got to know him because of this baby. Because of how important it is to him to have his own family. He lost his father when he was too young and he's still Nate's hero. His dad made him feel like he could be a hero, too, and you know what? That's exactly what he is. He doesn't just save lives in an emergency department—he gets on a helicopter and flies into places that make his job so much more difficult and he does it with an absolute passion for helping the people who need him the most. Any kid would think that a dad who did that was something special, wouldn't they?'

'He is special,' Simone agreed. 'That's why I chose to be a surrogate for him.' Her sigh was audible. 'And his wife.'

"Did you know how protective he's been of the baby you're carrying—ever since he knew you were pregnant? He was a real mess when his marriage fell apart because he was scared—really *scared*—that you might think he couldn't be the best parent if he was a single dad. He told me that if he lost the chance to be part of his child's life, it would haunt him forever.'

'That's something we've talked about.' Simone sounded more sure of herself now. 'Nate's the biological father of this child. We know he needs to be involved to some degree. We'll figure something out.'

Nate was leaning against the wall of the corridor right outside the door. He closed his eyes when he heard Simone say this. It was a small step towards acknowledging his rights as a father, but it wasn't enough. Not nearly enough.

'Did he tell you that it was Donna that ended the marriage? That she left him for a man that she's been having an affair with for maybe a couple of years? That she told him that the baby was only his so he could have it—by himself?'

Outside the door, Nate winced at the private revelation but could hear Simone's shocked gasp.

'No…he never told me any of that. But…she seemed to be just as keen to have a baby as he was. Was she lying to everybody?'

'Maybe she wasn't sure what she really wanted,' Alice suggested quietly. 'But when the reality hit that they had a child on the way, she realised what she really *didn't* want. And I think Nate realised just how much he *did* want exactly this.'

Simone was silent. The sniff Nate could hear from Alice revealed that she was struggling with tears and he had to press himself against the wall to resist the urge to go into the room and put his arms around her.

'I grew up without a father,' Alice said then. 'A few contenders for a stepfather but nothing ever worked out because none of them wanted someone else's kid. I never had anyone that wanted me that much. Not even my mother or my grandmother. I can't imagine what it would feel like to have someone want me as much as Nate wants his baby. Or who would love me the way he could. He's the most wonderful man, Simone. He's clever and kind and gentle and so…loyal. He bought that house you came to see us in because of the Wendy house in the garden. He painted the table and chairs in the brightest colours he could find. And now…' Alice's breath escaped in an almost sob. 'Now he won't see Daisy playing in it.'

'Daisy?'

'It's a family name. Nate's grandmother. I think that's what he would like his daughter to be called.'

There was a longer silence from Simone this time and then she spoke slowly. 'But that's the problem, don't you see? It's family that we want for this baby. Not for her to be raised by a single, working father and maybe an endless stream of nannies.'

'He didn't set out to be a single father,' Alice said. 'And he might well get married again one day, after his divorce comes through. What if…?' Her next words were whispered. 'What if *I* was there instead of a nanny?'

'You'd want to look after someone else's baby?'

'This isn't "someone else's" baby. This is *Nate's* baby. And yes… I'd love to help take care of her.'

She would, Alice realised. She could love that little baby if she was allowed to. As much as if it was her own. She'd never let Daisy feel unloved, not for a heartbeat.

'But you work full time, don't you?'

'I'm not the only person who would want to help. Aratika Rescue Base is full of people that think the world of Nate. We'd all help. I could cut back on my hours and juggle my rosters so I can fill in gaps when Nate can't be at home.'

'Why would you want to do that?'

'Because…' Alice cleared her throat. 'I love him. I'm never going to love anyone else the way I love Nate.'

'Does he know that?'

*He does now,* Nate thought. And it was giving him a warm glow that came from somewhere very deep and was now spreading right through his body, all the way to the tips of his fingers and toes. It was making him feel…*happy*. Safe. As though he could stop wishing for things he didn't have and simply be grateful for…*this*—something that most people dream of having.

He'd known he'd been in danger of falling in love with Alice but of course he hadn't known how she felt about him. Quite the opposite. That night when he'd invited her to stay, had she been running away from him because she thought she needed to hide how she felt? *Why?*

Was Alice shaking her head? Was that what was making her next words wobble?

'I haven't told him. It was too soon after his marriage had broken up. I knew that the only important thing in his life right now was his baby. He even said that to me and I knew that the last thing he needed was the complication of getting into another relationship. I thought it was the last thing *I* needed, to be honest. I was only trying to help him show you that he would be the best father ever, whether he has a partner or not. I… I didn't mean to fall in love with him but… I'll always be there for him, if he wants me…'

'Of course he wants you.' Simone sounded as if she was crying now. 'It's obvious how much in love you two are.' She made a frustrated sound. 'Sorry, but I have to go,' she said. 'I'm going to be late for my appointment.'

'Okay. I hope everything's fine. Take care, Simone. And…thank you for listening.'

'Tell Nate…no…don't say anything. Could you just ask him to call me later? This evening, when I've had a chance to talk to Olly.'

Alice ended the call.

Her lunch break was over but she didn't make a move to leave this on-call room yet. She needed a moment to try and breathe through the emotional aftermath of that intense conversation.

It wasn't easy. Because this was the room where she and Nate had given in to the overwhelming level of attraction between them and broken through the conventional boundaries of friendship. She could remember every touch. Every kiss. Every murmured word. Had she really thought that she had pulled the plug before she fell in love with Nathaniel Madden by sticking to a new boundary of not staying a whole night with him? She'd lost any control over that long before then, hadn't she?

Maybe it had been when he'd told her how much he'd wanted to protect his baby from the moment he knew she'd been conceived.

Or had it been when she'd seen that plea for help in his eyes and she'd known that, if it was humanly possible, she would give him anything he asked for?

The real crunch had been the baby, though, hadn't it? Nicole's baby. When she'd been hit with the realisation that she wanted her own baby.

She just hadn't dared to acknowledge that it wasn't simply a baby she wanted.

It was the whole package. A family.

And there was only one person she would ever choose to create that family with.

Nate…

It had only taken the space of time it took to draw in a single deep breath for her brain to process the flash of her thoughts and feelings. It was her body's turn to react a heartbeat later, as it jerked in alarm at the sound from just outside the door of this room.

A door that she hadn't realised she'd left open that far.

A door that was opening even further as she watched it.

Her jaw dropped as she saw who was stepping into the room.

'*Nate?* Oh, my God…how long have you been out there?'

'Long enough.'

Alice could feel the colour draining from her face. 'I wasn't trying to interfere,' she said. 'I'm sorry… I might have even made things worse but… I couldn't *not* try to help. Because… because…'

Nate was closing the gap between them. 'Because you love me?'

He looked as though he was trying to smile but it wasn't quite working. The intensity in his eyes was overpowering anything else his face wanted to do. He was close enough to touch Alice now but he was simply standing there, in front of her.

'I love you, too,' he said. 'I've never felt like this about anyone. Ever. You're the best friend I've ever had. The best colleague. The absolutely best lover.' His lips curled a little but the embryonic smile faded just as fast. 'I knew I was pushing things further than you were comfortable with when I asked you to stay the night with me but, if I'm honest, that's what I want—every night for the rest of my life. I want to wake up and find you beside me every morning for the rest of my life.'

'But I'm not what's important right now,' Alice said, with a gulp. 'What matters most is Daisy.'

Incredibly, Nate's head made a side-to-side movement to contradict her.

'What matters most right now,' he said softly, 'is you, Alice Barlow. It was you who gave me the confidence to step up to being a single dad and get my life sorted. Who let me see that future I'd dreamed of by reminding me of what that Wendy house represented. It was you who gave me the strength and focus to do my job when there was a case where we could have lost a mother and baby and that could have derailed me.' He was really smiling now. 'It was you who reminded me of how much I loved my dad and how much I want to be like him for my own child. How much I want a family.'

Nate closed his eyes for a long blink as he took a new breath. And then he opened them again.

'You make me the best person I could be,' he added. 'And I need you in my life. In my family.' He was pulling Alice into his arms, now. 'You *are* my family.' His voice was raw. 'But I couldn't tell you that, not just because it's taken this long for me to see what's been in front of me all along but because of what you said that night you discovered that you hated Guinness.'

A huff of laughter escaped Alice.

'Do you remember what it was?'

She bit her lip. 'You mean about life being perfect with having no family at all? Or was it the bit about not wanting kids?'

Nate held her tighter by way of response. Was he holding his breath?

She looked up so that he could see her face properly. Her heart was hammering against her ribs.

This was it.

The moment where she could reach for a totally new future, if she was brave enough.

'You're not the only one who can go a long time with not seeing what's in front of you,' she told him. 'I've spent my whole life, ever since I gave that doll away to the girl down the street, believing that children are the last thing I would ever want. But you know when I saw the truth?'

'Yeah…' Nate's lips were on her hair. 'It was when you were holding Nicole's baby, wasn't it?'

Alice nodded.

'I knew the truth then, too, but I wasn't sure if you would believe it.'

The love Alice knew she had for this man was already filling her heart to bursting but this made it overflow.

She hadn't been ready to believe it then. He knew her *that* well. He understood just how huge that had been. He was always going to be there for her, just the way she would be for him. Helping her to be a better person than she could ever be without him.

There was so much she wanted to say but there were only three words that escaped her lips.

The ones that mattered the most.

'I love you…'

# EPILOGUE

*Three years later...*

'HAPPY ANNIVERSARY, DARLING.'

Alice Madden turned her head sharply, to where her husband was sitting beside her on a rustic wooden bench in the garden, her eyes wide with surprise. 'Oh, no…have I forgotten something important?'

Nate smiled at her. 'Think about it.'

Oh…the *love* in that smile…

Whatever it was, it had to be something to do with what Nathaniel loved most in the world—his family. Alice turned her gaze to where Daisy was playing on the veranda of the Wendy house, sitting on the top step with her tea set arranged around her chubby little legs.

It was only water in the teapot but Daisy was pouring it into the little plastic cup as if everything depended on not spilling a drop. It was too much of a challenge to get to her feet, holding the bright red cup without slopping water over the edge but Daisy didn't seem to mind. She was on her way from the Wendy house steps towards the wooden bench that Nate had built under the pohutukawa tree, a triumphant smile on her face.

'It's not Daisy's birthday,' Alice said. 'That's two months away. Oh…did I tell you that Simone's coming up for the party? She said there was no way she was going to miss Daisy's third birthday—especially when it's a princess party. She's borrowed a crown from the kids' dress-up box and Olly's going to look after the kids for the night.'

'That man's a hero,' Nate said.

'He is,' Alice agreed. 'I will love him forever for standing back and letting you cut Daisy's umbilical cord.'

*You're her father*, he'd told Nate. *You need to do this.*

They'd arrived only minutes before Daisy made her appearance, after a mad dash to the airport and the assistance of people who knew them both from their work at Aratika. Someone in the control tower actually paused a plane from beginning to taxi out for take-off so that the air bridge could be opened again and allow two extra passengers on board. Nobody on the flight minded being held up. The pilot had apparently told them they were waiting for a dad who desperately wanted to be at his daughter's birth and they all clapped as Nate and Alice came aboard.

Olly was also a hero for whispering in Simone's ear not long after that, when Nate was holding his daughter for the first time and the medical staff were happy to leave the room, and he made the suggestion that saw him help his wife into a wheelchair and push her out of the room to leave Nate, Alice and baby Daisy alone for those first precious minutes of bonding as a brand new family.

Nearly three years ago. And here she was coming towards her parents, a very happy and healthy little girl. Nate was watching her progress across the lawn. His daughter was watching him. Her smile widened and she was walking faster. She didn't seem to notice that more water had gone over the edge of the red cup.

'Cuppa tea,' she announced proudly as she got closer.

'Oh, thank you…' Alice reached out her hand but Daisy shook her head. 'For Dadda,' she said firmly.

Alice wasn't the least bit offended. She laughed aloud. 'You're such a daddy's girl,' she told Daisy. She threw Nate a sideways glance. 'Like me…' she murmured.

Nate winked at Alice but then gave his daughter his full attention as he gravely accepted the cup. There couldn't have been more than a teaspoon of water in the bottom by now but he made an impressive slurping noise as he pretended to drink it.

'That's the best cup of tea I think I've ever had,' he said.

Daisy beamed.

'Do you think Mumma might like one as well?'

Daisy nodded. She took the cup from Nate and turned around to toddle back to where her teapot was.

Alice was still smiling but she shook her head.

'It's not our wedding anniversary,' she said. 'We haven't even got to six months yet and I don't think either of us are going to forget our first anniversary.'

Nate let his breath out in a contented sigh. 'I'll never forget that day,' he vowed. He reached to pick up Alice's hand. 'That moment when I was standing right here, under this tree, and you came around the corner of the house and down the path in your wedding dress I knew that I was marrying the most beautiful woman in the world and that made me the happiest man on the planet.'

'And I was the happiest woman.' Alice echoed his sigh. 'And wasn't Daisy the cutest flower girl ever? The way she stopped every few steps and stared into her little basket and then picked out one rose petal at a time and had to crouch down to put it so carefully on the ground.'

She'd been wearing a pink dress that had flowers and butterflies embroidered on it. It had little pink wings attached to the back of it and there'd been a halo of flowers in Daisy's soft, dark curls.

She'd sat at their feet, taking out the rest of the rose petals, one at a time, from the basket, as Nate and Alice had exchanged their heartfelt vows and the rings.

'She was adorable,' Nate agreed.

Everybody would have agreed with that. Especially the celebrant. She'd just pronounced them husband and wife when Daisy discarded her basket, got to her feet and held out her arms.

'Up,' she commanded.

In Nate's arms a moment later, the celebrant had joined in the laughter of all the guests and pronounced them a family as well.

But, however wonderful those memories were, it wasn't what Nate was referring to.

'I'm good with dates,' Alice protested. 'What am I missing that's special enough for you to remember?'

'To be honest,' Nate admitted, 'I wouldn't have remembered this particular date if I hadn't upgraded my phone yesterday.'

Alice blinked. 'What's that got to do with it?'

'I was deleting some old photographs and messages.' Nate took his phone out of his pocket and swiped the screen. 'And I found this.' He handed the phone to Alice.

It was a text conversation that had happened, three years ago today, between Nate and Simone. Alice hadn't ever seen this even though she'd been sitting with Nate as it happened. She'd been too focused on watching his face and then too overwhelmed with the joy of its conclusion to ever ask to see exactly what had been said. Nate had sent the first message.

The signal's terrible. The call won't go through. Are you okay to text?

Yes. All good.

I have to confess—it was unintentional but I overheard Alice talking to you.

She loves you.

I know. I love her just as much.

I knew that. Have you told her?

Yes.

Does she want this baby as much as you do?

Yes. Absolutely.

I've talked to Olly. We think you're going to make a perfect family. We'll both be happy to sign the consent when it comes time for Daisy's adoption.

I can't tell you how happy I am.

I know. I also know that the love you have for each other is strong enough to last a lifetime. Never forget that, will you?

I won't. I promise.

Alice didn't need to read the sign-off and arrangement to talk again soon. The words had blurred, anyway, and she was blinking as she handed the phone back to Nate.

'It's a date we should both remember from now on,' she said, leaning her head against Nate's shoulder. 'That was really the day we became a family, wasn't it?'

'It was.' Nate's arm went around her back to hold her against him.

They were both watching Daisy, who had finished pouring the second cup of 'tea' and was getting unsteadily to her feet. Most of the water was spilling.

'Just as well,' Nate muttered. 'That tea tasted a bit funny.'

Alice laughed but then stopped suddenly, with a tiny gasp.

'What?' Nate's head swerved. 'Is something wrong?'

'No…' Alice reached for his other hand and placed it, palm down, on her belly. 'I think I just felt the first real kick.'

She was only just beginning to show in this pregnancy and this was a real milestone.

'Did you feel that?'

Nate didn't need to say anything. He looked up and caught Alice's gaze and she could see tears shining in his eyes.

Tears of joy.

'Mumma…' Daisy called. 'Here I come…'

But Alice was still holding Nate's gaze. 'Simone was right,' she said. 'I'm so glad I've got a lifetime to love you.'

Nate was leaning in to kiss her, his hand still on her belly. 'Me, too,' he whispered.

* * * * *

*Look out for the next story in*
*the Aratika Air Rescue Trilogy*
*Coming soon!*
*And if you enjoyed this story, check out these*
*other great reads from Alison Roberts*

Single Dad for the Daredevil Doctor
A Family Made in the ER
Single Dad's Christmas Wish

*All available now!*